Clinton Scollard

A Man-at-arms

A Romance of the Days of Gian Galeazzo Visconti, the Great Viper

Clinton Scollard

A Man-at-arms

A Romance of the Days of Gian Galeazzo Visconti, the Great Viper

ISBN/EAN: 9783744764261

Printed in Europe, USA, Canada, Australia, Japan

Cover: Foto ©Andreas Hilbeck / pixelio.de

More available books at **www.hansebooks.com**

"Was I not the trusted messenger of a great lord?" — Page 54

A Man-at-Arms

A Romance of the Days of Gian Galeazzo Visconti, the Great Viper

By

Clinton Scollard

Illustrated by

E. W. D. Hamilton

Lamson, Wolffe and Company

Boston, New York and London

M DCCC XCVIII

To

Irving Gilmore Brown

Contents

Chapter		Page
I.	I part Company with my Father	1
II.	I encounter Gian Galeazzo Visconti	8
III.	I enter the Service of the Lord of Pavia	23
IV.	The Proving of a Guardsman	34
V.	My First Outriding	49
VI.	In a Brescia Garden	64
VII.	A Night at the Two Falcons	82
VIII.	The Mission to Milan	103
IX.	The Coup-de-Main	127
X.	The Last March of Bernabo	136
XI.	The Face at the Casement	148
XII.	At Padua	161
XIII.	The Affair of the Via San Lorenzo	188
XIV.	I have Some Last Words with my Father	204
XV.	The Black Closet	227
XVI.	To the Rescue	242

Contents

Chapter		Page
XVII.	The Encounter at Como	259
XVIII.	Up the Lake	272
XIX.	The Tower of Vezio	287
XX.	The Flight by Night	309
XXI.	The House of the Canari	323
XXII.	Out of the Viper's Coils	343

List of Illustrations

Opposite Page

"Was I not the trusted messenger of a great lord?" . . . . *Frontispiece*

"For some reason these three men were endeavoring to draw me out" . . . 63

The Signorina Angela Canaro . . 75

The Death of the Master of the Hounds . 146

"Bidding one go in search of a reputable leech" 196

"There was no need of words of wooing" . 308

A Man-at-Arms

Chapter I

I part Company with my Father

I DESCENDED slowly and with the greatest caution, hugging my sword to my hip so that it might not clash upon the stair. I had no stomach for an encounter with my father, and hoped to pass the entrance to his room of retirement unobserved, but this was not to be. The door was ajar, and my shadow fell upon the floor. As he looked up from the parchment over which he was bending, his eyes rested first upon my plumed cap, and then ran swiftly over my whole accoutrement, my gay trunks, my slashed doublet, and the taffeta-lined cloak which hung from my shoulder. Gradually his face darkened until it became a hue quite in keeping with the black velvet skull-cap he had recently taken to wearing to protect his sparsely thatched poll from draughts.

"Whither go you, Luigi?" he asked, in his most incisive way.

"To the river promenade," I answered.

"With whom consort you there?"

"With my friends, Andrea Campiglione and Paolo Smeraldi," I said; for I would not deceive him, though I knew that his anger would take flame at my reply.

"It is with such, then, that you choose to associate despite my wishes!" my father exclaimed. "Bravos, swashbucklers; nay, for aught I know, worse!"

"Hold!" he continued, rising, and checking the speech that leaped to my lips. "I have something more to say to you, sir, but not in your brother's presence. Leave us, Rinaldo."

My stripling half-brother, who had been construing his task in Latin, shuffled from the room with ill grace, glowering at my father, whom he strongly resembled and whose favorite he was, and casting at me a look in which I read a gleeful malice.

Truth to say, my home was little to my liking, fine though it was as any in all Pavia. I was heir by birth to my father's house, had just entered upon my twenty-third year, and was but two weeks returned from the completion of my studies at the University of Bologna, yet I was made to feel like a stranger under an alien roof. My stepmother had always looked upon me as a barrier to her own child's advancement, and it was owing to her dislike for me, which she was at no pains to conceal, that I was kept much of the time from home.

Between my father and myself, too, I had discovered when I returned to Pavia year after year, during the long break in the university session, there was a growing lack of sympathy. One day I had turned to him suddenly, and found him regarding me with a curious intentness. In answer to my question as to the reason for his scrutiny he said he was reading my mother's looks in my face, and from his expression I saw that he was little pleased thereat. This fact I pondered upon

much, and took occasion, not long afterward, to entreat him to tell me something
of my mother, who had died a year after
my birth, and concerning whom I knew
almost nothing save that she came of a
noble Paduan family.

I got little satisfaction from him, however, and gradually a suspicion dawned
upon me that the memory of my mother
was for some reason not pleasant to him,
and that the growing resemblance to her
which he saw in me made me distasteful
in his sight. Then our likings were radi-
cally different. I had small fancy for
jurisprudence, in which it was his special
desire that I should excel, and had ambitions of a soldierly character which he per-
sistently frowned upon.

My father said nothing until Rinaldo's
footsteps had died away down the wide
hall. Then he took from the table a
letter which he unfolded and began scanning, his brow contracting as he did so.

"This," he said, shaking the script
almost in my face, "has come to me from
Bologna to-day."

I strove to look unconcerned, but my effort was a failure, and my father saw my uneasiness. That the writing in some way referred to my bouts at arms I had no doubt, affairs which I had previously succeeded in keeping from his ears.

"Perhaps you would like to hear what my correspondent, one of your preceptors, has to say?" he continued.

I saw that he was working himself into a fury, and remained silent.

"Listen to this," he cried, and began reading, his voice tremulous with passion: "While your son's scholarly attainments fall, I fear, far short of what you might wish, he being but a poor lover of his books, his skill at arms (an art in these days vastly more to a man's profit than that of the scribe) is, if common rumor may be believed, likely to bring him to great renown. His exploits have been, and are long likely to be, the talk of the University."

"You are doubtless proud of your record!" exclaimed my father bitterly, as he lifted his eyes from the paper. Then something in my demeanor, in the expression of my features, drew a great oath from him.

"Body of Christ!" said he, "don't look at me like that, or I shall take you by the throat. That was the very air your mother wore when I told her she had a lover."

"What!" I cried, moved to speech for the first time, and scarcely crediting my ears.

"Yes," said he, "that accursed mixture of resentment and pride and injured innocence."

"My mother had a lover!" I exclaimed, not heeding his last words. "Sir, if that be true, why do you, my father, now cast it in my teeth?"

"Because you, like her in voice, in feature, in every motion, have, like her, never once during your lifetime carried out my wishes, and have now come back to me a bravo, a brawler, a picker of street quarrels, to disgrace me as she did."

I know not how I restrained myself at this most unjust and unnatural outburst;

for it seemed to me if man ever deserved to be spitted without remorse it was this creature before me, whom I had always called father; yet, though my blood surged hot within me, I replied to him evenly.

"Sir," I said, "I believe you foully slander my mother's memory, and never will I again set foot beneath your roof until you recall those base words. As for what you say in regard to myself, if I now become that which you accuse me of being, it will be your doing and not mine."

This said, my father almost frothing with rage the while, and yet not daring to lay hands on me, I wheeled about, strode through the hallway, and down the main staircase to the court, taking no pains now to hug my sword to my hip, but letting it clash upon the stones as I went, and glorying in the angry echoes that swarmed about my ears.

Chapter II

I encounter Gian Galeazzo Visconti

I FOUND my three companions await-ing me by the river gate, whither I went like one walking in his sleep. They at once saw by my manner that something untoward had taken place, and began to rally me, thinking that the loss of a smile, or the withdrawal of a fond look from a pair of dark eyes, had caused my perturbation. I took no pains to cor-rect this impression, but told them that they would have to go their ways without me that evening, as I was in no mood for gallantries. This gave strength to the notion that I was vexed by an unlucky love affair, and I parted from them amid a chorus of fleers that did not tend to make me any the more amiable.

Along the Via Ticino I took my way, turning neither to the right nor to the left, going to the wall for no one, much to the wrath of many good citizens who were out for an airing after the employment of the day. Quarrels had there been in plenty had I chosen to accept them, and under ordinary circumstances (I now confess it with shame) I would not have been backward. And yet in justice to myself I should say that it was far from my custom to flaunt it so heedlessly through the streets, regardless of the rights of others.

My wrath against my father mounted as I went on, and I took a resolve that it should be my mission to probe to the bottom his accusation against my mother, and force him to retract his foul slander upon her good name, for that she could be guilty of what he had averred never for an instant entered my mind. Before my purpose could be effected, however, I must find a means of livelihood. I cast aside at once all thought of continuing in the course my father had mapped out for me, which was to end in an advocateship and judgeship, and determined to enter the profession which then offered the quickest means of advancement, and the one for which I well knew I was best fitted, — that of arms.

It was not for naught, I now told myself, that I had given more attention to books on military tactics than to those upon jurisprudence ; that I had frequented the fencing-halls more assiduously than the lecture-rooms ; that I knew the masters of fence (drawn to Bologna from all Europe) more intimately than the learned professors of the University.

I realized that, with my knowledge of sword-practice, it would not be difficult for me to find a place in one of the many companies maintained by the overlords of the chief Italian cities. But to serve as a common soldier, a mere underling, was far from my ambition. Yet, better that, I said to myself, than the life I had seen opening before me in my father's house.

To whom should I offer myself? As this question came to my mind for decision I emerged from the Via Ticino, and found myself in the wide open space in front of the Palazzo Visconti. Two German guards in their dark jerkins stood, pikes in hand, at the entrance gateway. I seemed to read in them an answer to my question. And yet for good reasons I hesitated to apply to Gian Galeazzo, the head of the branch of the Visconti who held the over-lordship of Pavia. True, rumor had it that he was anxious for recruits to swell the company he was forming, but there had never been a feeling of great friend-liness between my family and the Visconti because we were allied, although not closely, with the Beccaria, whose rule in Pavia the Visconti had overthrown.

Could I have had my choice, I would have sought out some of the members of my mother's house in Padua (for though my mother was an orphan, and reared by an uncle, I felt that there must be some of her kin still living) and there taken service under Francesco da Carrara. But how could I, with only a few florins in my pocket, and with no gear save that upon my back, expect to be able to make so

extended a journey, and establish my identity among those whom I had never seen?
No, at present Padua could not be thought
of, and under Gian Galeazzo's uncle, Bernabo, who held sway at Milan, I would
not serve, for I knew him to be a cruel
and detestable tyrant. I might possibly
manage to reach Mantua, where the family
of Gonzaga held supremacy, and it was
with the idea of deciding whether I should
attempt to do this, or should approach
Gian Galeazzo, that I crossed the piazza in
front of the palace, and passed through the
gateway of Santa Maria in Portica into the
open country.

The sun was low on the horizon, and
the laborers were plodding homeward
from the fields. I doubt not they cast
many curious glances at me, for a young
gallant in my array was a rare sight on
foot upon the highway, and I went along
with down-bent head and no eyes for
those whom I passed. I had gone some
distance between the fields and orchards,
and was approaching a small tributary of
the Ticino, called the Vernavola, when I

heard the clatter of horses' hoofs. Who the approaching horseman was I could not see, for the thoroughfare curved abruptly just beyond where a bridge spanned the stream, and here was a group of poplars. Moreover, the stream was fringed by a growth of underbrush, and on both sides of it were mulberry orchards.

Louder grew the sound of the hoof-beats, and ere the horse and rider came into view, I heard the animal's labored breathing. It was evident that some one spurred in haste. Around the bend and across the bridge plunged the steed, head stretched forward and nostrils wide. He who rode held the bridle nervelessly, and was crouching low, clutching the saddle. His cloak had been partly torn loose, and flapped out upon his left like a great wing. His head was uncovered, and his hair blew about his colorless face. I had stepped aside upon the sward to let him pass, and he shot at me an apprehensive glance as he swept by. A stride beyond where I stood the horse stumbled, and the uncertain rider was thrown from the saddle and cast heavily on the turf at the road edge. The animal recovered itself, and raced Pavia-ward, riderless. As I hastened to the assistance of the fallen man, I noted for the first time that there were other horsemen approaching, and it flashed upon me that they were in pursuit.

"Are you much hurt, sir?" I cried, assisting the unfortunate horseman to his feet.

"Mother of Christ, is there no escape?" said he, without heeding my anxious inquiry, casting about him a glance of terror and despair, as though he would fain discover some place whither he could fly.

It was then that I recognized him, though I had not set eyes upon him for several years, and he seemed to have changed much in the interval, his face now being thinner and more ascetic. The man before me was none other than the ruler of Pavia, Gian Galeazzo Visconti, and he was in some mortal peril. Was ever youth anxious to win the favor of one in high place more fortunate in his opportunity! I realized that Fate had thrown in my path the golden apple of chance, and I was not slow to grasp it.

"You are pursued,— your life is in danger!" I exclaimed, the iron hoofs of the nearing horses seeming so to terrify the man before me that he was incapable of action or further speech. "Come!" I seized him by the arm as I said this, and dragged him toward the stone barrier which separated the highway from the mulberry orchard. I had to assist him in crossing the wall, so stiff and bruised was he, and we had barely time to crouch in the drainage ditch upon the other side when the adjoining bridge rang with the passage of several horsemen. I knew that they would at once discover the riderless steed of Gian Galeazzo, and that they would doubtless rein their animals, and begin to search for the missing fugitive. Could we reach the undergrowth skirting the Vernavola before they turned and began their search, I felt that we had a very good chance of escaping unobserved.

"Quick!" I whispered to my companion, forgetting, in the stress of events, to
address him by any title of respect; "we
must follow this ditch to the stream."

Exclamations of chagrin and anger,
mingled with cries of command to the
horses, came to us, as we started, from a
short distance down the road.

I had heard many times that the Lord
of Pavia was a coward, and precious little
show of bravery did he exhibit in this
emergency. I could hear his teeth chattering as he crept along behind me, and
when we at length reached the cover of
the underbrush on the banks of the Vernavola the perspiration stood in great
drops on his forehead, and he sank upon
the ground, shaking with fear. I made
haste to peer from our concealment and
found the horsemen, three in number, had
halted their steeds, and were narrowly
scanning the adjacent fields and orchards.
It was evident that they had no suspicion
of the fugitive's whereabouts.

While I was thus engaged in recon-
noitring, the Visconti clutched my arm.

He was still in a tremor, and his breath came in gasps.

"Have they seen us?" he whispered apprehensively.

"No," I returned, "and if we hasten, there is small chance that they will, but we must be cautious not to stir the undergrowth so as to attract their attention."

He let me lead the way, saying as he did so, —

"I am not one who forgets a service such as you have rendered me!"

The hunted, terrified look died from his eyes, and a flush of color gave a more agreeable expression to his pasty face.   I saw that he was beginning to consider that the danger had passed, as indeed it had, for by the time the three horsemen decided to beat the bushes which fringed the Vernavola we were well out of their clutches.

At length we reached a sunken laneway which led through the fields in the direction of the high-road.

"It is perfectly safe to follow this," I said; "your Lordship is quite out of danger."

He stopped abruptly, and gave me a curious look.

"You know me, then!" he exclaimed. "I thought you did not. Your face is not familiar to me. Are you a Pavian?"

"I am," I answered, "and am called Luigi della Verria." Then, thinking he might be displeased at the abrupt way in which I had addressed him when he was in peril by the roadway bridge, I added, "I trust your Lordship will pardon my peremptory words a few moments since. I was so anxious for your safety that my manners left me."

I could see that this pleased him, for he replied with a smile, —

"There is naught to pardon, for assuredly had it not been for your readiness to command, my carcass might even now be food for prowling curs or the minnows of this very stream."

He had quite recovered his wonted serenity, and spoke almost gayly as we plodded toward the road, yet I noted that his manner was more that of the scholar,

or even the churchman, than that of the
man of affairs.

"Doubtless I have to thank my excellent uncle, Bernabo, for this lively bit of
entertainment!" he exclaimed. "By our
Lady, young sir," he continued, "I would
that I had a fearless spirit like yours in
this poor body of mine!"

"But I was in no danger," I said,
making what excuse I could for his lack
of courage.

"Do you think those villains would
have spared you," cried he, "if they had
discovered you while assisting me to
escape? They would have hacked us
down as they did my poor troopers
yonder."

"There were places by the stream
where we might have made a very pretty
defence," said I. "Two pitted against
three are not at such a grievous disadvantage."

"You speak with confidence as though
you were accustomed to sword-play."

I saw him look at me with increasing
interest as he said this.

" I am not without some trifling experience," I replied.

We were now very near the high-road,
and our conversation was cut short by the
appearance of a dozen troopers riding
hastily from the direction of the city.
Their leader caught sight of Gian Galeazzo,
and drew rein abruptly, commanding his
men to halt. Then he dismounted, and
doffing his cap of steel came toward us.

" We were much disturbed about your
Lordship's safety," he said brokenly, with
a strong German accent. "Your steed
rushed into the palace court riderless,
whereat we immediately mounted and set
out to discover what had happened."

" You did well," the Lord of Pavia
answered him, speaking in German. " I
was sore beset, and had it not been for
the assistance of this young gentleman I
should not now be telling of my adventure.
I went for my evening ride with three
of your comrades, as you know. Just
beyond the hamlet of Vernavola we were
suddenly attacked by seven mounted men,
who spurred upon us from behind a farm-

stead wall. My guard made a gallant defence, enabling me to break away from the press, and although pursued, I feel sure that I should have escaped on horseback had my animal not stumbled and thrown me. It was then, when my pursuers were close on me, that this young man, who chanced to be at hand, assisted me in eluding the villains."

"It was little that I did," I said, thinking now to take my leave of him, for one of the troopers had dismounted, and the Visconti had put his hand upon the pommel of the vacant saddle. "But I pray your Lordship to believe that I would do him any service with the same cheerfulness."

"Ah!" he exclaimed, as I was about withdrawing, resolved that on the morrow I would present myself to him and ask to be taken into his service, "you understand the German tongue!"

"Yes," I replied, "I had some acquaintances among the Germans at the University of Bologna."

"Now that you speak of Bologna, I

recall to have heard that Giovanni della Verria had a son at the University."

"I am he."

I bowed, and made as though I would retire.

"Stay!" he said, "I would have some further words with you.   Will you not ride back to the city with me?"

Here was an invitation which it would have been gross folly to refuse; another trooper was commanded to dismount, and I who had left Pavia little more than an hour since, a self-elected outcast from my father's house, rode back by the side of the most powerful man within its walls, Gian Galeazzo Visconti.

Chapter III

ERE we reached the gateway of Santa Maria in Portica, the red afterglow had faded from the sky. If the Lord of Pavia had in mind any special matter concerning which he desired to speak with me, he certainly did not broach it during the ride, though he talked freely on general topics, and I was not so blind as not to realize that he was drawing me out, for during our conversation he put to me several keen and searching questions.

We rode into the palace courtyard amid a glare of torches, and a buzz of many voices. A tall soldierly figure strode out from a group of men-at-arms and greeted Gian Galeazzo heartily, and after the Lord of Pavia had issued several orders which did not reach my ears, these two went into the palace together.

Though I had not been dismissed, I took it for granted that his Lordship had nothing more to say to me that evening, and was making my way toward the gateway through the crowd of troopers who thronged the courtyard, when some one plucked my sleeve. I turned and found that it was the leader of the band who had gone out in search of the Visconti.

"His Lordship wishes me to tell you," the soldier said, "that if it is your pleasure to remain for a little he will speak further with you."

"My time is at his disposal," I replied.

"Very good. If you will follow me, I will show you where you are to wait."

I was conducted along partially finished hallways (the palace being incomplete, as it had been left by Galeazzo, the former Lord of Pavia, he who had married his daughter Violante to Clarence, son of Edward III. of England, and brother of the Black Prince, with such pomp and prodigality), and finally ushered into a small, but tastefully appointed waiting-room. For a space I found my own thoughts very agreeable company. Certainly, I told myself, this attention on the part of Gian Galeazzo boded well for me. Then I began to review what I knew in regard to the man into whose service I hoped to enter. I judged him to be approaching forty years of age. He had been twice married, his first wife having been Isabella of Valois, daughter of King John of France. She it was who brought him, as part of her dowry, the county of Virtus in Champagne, from which he was sometimes called Count Virtu. His second wife, with whom he was now living, was Caterina, his cousin, the daughter of Bernabo Visconti, Lord of Milan. He had been overlord of Pavia since his father's death seven years previous, in 1378. He had the reputation of being just and lenient in his rule, and I recalled that I had heard my father, who bore the family no good will, commend him for the reforms which he had carried into effect. It was common rumor that he was learned, and that he affected to be pious, for he spent much time with the clergy and men of religious orders. He made no secret of his lack of physical strength and bravery, but this was usually set down to his delicate constitution, and was not looked upon as condemnatory of his character. On the whole he was respected, even liked, by the populace, who contrasted with words of praise his mild sway with that of his irascible father, and with that of his cruel uncle in Milan.

That Gian Galeazzo was slowly and without ostentation, in fact with as much secrecy as possible, forming a formidable military company was a matter of considerable wonder, and not a little discussion, among the citizens of Pavia. It had always been the custom for the overlords of the city to keep at call a small yet efficient body of guardsmen, but the number of soldiers that Gian Galeazzo had gathered about him far outnumbered any previous band. That a man of the supposed character of the present Lord should embark upon any military enterprise appeared most unlikely, and it began to be whispered that Bernabo, Galeazzo's uncle, had designs upon Pavia, and that his nephew did not propose to be taken unaware. The Pavians had no desire to come under the sway of the Milan tyrant, consequently the soldiers were not looked upon with disfavor, despite the fact that most of them were aliens, the largest number being Germans. The command and organization of the company had been given to the noted *condittiere*, Jacobo del Verme.

I had heard these matters talked over in the streets, and though much interested in them, had restrained myself from visiting the quarters of the soldiers, and had shunned the vicinity of the palace, where many of them were constantly to be seen, because of the well-known antipathy of my father toward things military. Though he did not wish me to be ignorant of the use of the sword, it was under protest that I carried one, and it was partly because my two most intimate acquaintances were youths of spirit, who had been prominent in some affair which had come to his ears, that my father burst upon me in the tirade that led to our parting.

After a time I grew weary of conjecturing what the coming interview might have in store for me, and began to listen impatiently for the footstep of the one who should summon me into the presence of the Lord of Pavia. But the passages gave forth no sound, and I was constrained to attempt to study out the allegorical fresco upon the walls of the apartment in order to allay my nervous impatience. However, the flickering taper, which was the sole light within the room, shed so uncertain a glow that I finally gave up in disgust, and fell to watching a foolish moth that was hovering perilously near the wavering flame. When I had seen this poor atom fall, singed and twitching, to the floor, and had keyed my ear for the hundredth time for the desired sound in vain, I began to believe that I had been forgotten, and was meditating making my way back to the courtyard, when the door opposite the one by which I had entered swung back, and a page bade me follow him.

We crossed a stately reception-hall hung with rich tapestries and decorated with burnished mirrors, traversed a short passage, at the further end of which we halted where a dark curtain was swung. Upon the panelling behind this my guide tapped, and in response to a reply from within admitted me to a brightly illumined closet where two men were seated. One was the Lord of Pavia, and the other was he of the soldierly figure who had greeted Gian Galeazzo so warmly on his return.

The Visconti looked at me pleasantly as I made my obeisance.

"This gentleman," he said, turning to his companion, "is the commander of my guards and troops, Jacopo del Verme."

I saluted the noted soldier, and expressed the honor I felt in being presented to him. His face was bronzed and seamed with exposure. He had a muscular figure, and his alert eyes and resourceful mien bespoke the commander of men, one accustomed to be obeyed. I was far more impressed by him than by the Lord of Pavia, who had changed his stained and torn riding-costume for a sedate garb which suited him well, and yet which gave him the air of an advocate rather than that of a ruler of cities. The countenance of Gian Galeazzo Visconti was not one that inspired trust, although in those days he strove to win the confidence of all with whom he came in contact. There was a lack of warmth in his nature which showed in the expression of his eyes. Yet he simulated an ease and openness which, at the outset of an acquaintance with him, effectually hid the cunning and calculating depths of his heart. I was not drawn toward him as I was toward the hale and weather-beaten *condittiere*, and yet I was disposed to like him notwithstanding the fact that I could not forget his want of manliness in the affair of the high-road.

When Jacopo del Verme had looked me up and down in his sharp and critical fashion until I began to feel a desire to find a corner into which I could crawl and hide myself, he broke out abruptly, —

"His Lordship has taken a fancy to you, my young sir, without consideration of the fact that you have rendered him a notable service, and it would greatly please him if he could in some way attach you to his person."

He paused as though expecting me to make some reply, but I was too much perturbed by his scrutiny and his abrupt speech to answer at once, so he went on, thinking presumably that I wished to hear just what the Lord of Pavia might propose.

"There is a lieutenancy vacant in the palace guard which his Lordship thinks you might fill, but before offering you this there are three things to be considered: first, your own desire; second, your father's wish or consent; and third, your ability to fill the post."

"I thank his Lordship most heartily," I answered, now quite myself, "for the great honor which his proposal does me, and would say frankly that to serve him is my first wish. My father need not be taken into account in the matter, since he and I have parted company, and his desire would not weigh with me. As regards my ability to meet the requirements of the position in question, I hope to be able to prove both to his Lordship's satisfaction, and yours, that I am fully capable of doing so. I trust," I said, "that a lieutenant in the palace guard is not compelled to remain behind, if, by any chance, there is active service in the field."

Del Verme broke into a loud chuckle at this.

"I like your spirit!" cried he, "but you need have no fear of inactivity if you can satisfactorily show you are capable of filling the place for which his Lordship intends you."

"We will talk further of this on the morrow," said Gian Galeazzo. "I hope until that time, and indeed until this matter can be decided, that you will be my guest. I infer that such an arrangement will not be unacceptable to you, for I take it for granted from your reference to your father that you are no longer living at home."

I assented with expressions of gratitude to his Lordship's proposal that I abide at the palace, and having bidden him and Del Verme good night, followed the page, who was now summoned, to a sleeping-apartment in another portion of the great building. Here a serving-man brought me a light refreshment of spiced cakes and wine, and here, after the exciting scenes of the evening had slipped by slow degrees from my brain, I passed a restful night, although companioned by many dreams.

D

Chapter IV

The Proving of a Guardsman

I WAS awakened the next morning by a stir in the courtyard upon which the single window of my apartment looked, and rose hurriedly to see what was taking place. I found several groups of men-at-arms had gathered, many lackeys were hurrying to and fro, and in and out through the palace gateway was passing a stream of soldiers of all conditions. Ashamed that I had so overslept, I hastened to dress myself. Before I had finished, the serving-man who had waited upon me the night before entered, bearing my breakfast. He announced that his Lordship would see me sometime late in the morning, and that in the meanwhile he hoped I would amuse myself among the soldiers in the courtyard.

When I had eaten, I made way, although not without considerable perplexity, owing to the deviousness of the hallways, to the open air.   A bustling scene met my eyes as I halted a moment in the doorway before mingling with the soldiery.   The appearance of the place was that of a camp before battle, rather than that of the courtyard of a Signor supposedly at peace with his neighbors.   Some of the men were burnishing their steel headpieces, others their body armor; some were sharpening their lances or pikes, others were putting a keener edge on their swords.   Laughter and jests and oaths added to the noise of weapons and armor.   The guttural German, the vivacious French, and our own mellow speech blended in a curious and bewildering medley.

I was peering about among the various groups, endeavoring to catch a glimpse of the German officer whose acquaintance I had made on the previous evening, when my presence was noticed by half a dozen troopers who were lounging quite near, seemingly more idle than the rest.

"Good morrow, Sir Pretty Clothes!" called one of them, his accent betraying his northland birth.

Though I had been thoughtful enough to leave my gay cloak behind, and to put off some of my other finery, I realized that my fashionable attire was inappropriate for the hour and place, and so answered this greeting with perfect good nature.

"See him smile!" cried another of the troopers, speaking in German. "Is he not like a puppet in a booth? You pull a string, and he rolls his eyes to heaven; you pull another, and he smirks for you most maiden-like."

"By St. Christopher!" a third exclaimed, in the same tongue, "it is maiden-like he is. Look at those cheeks. Apricots have not a lovelier flush, and as for the hair, many a maid would be envious of that gold."

"Gold!" shouted he who had spoken first, moving toward me, followed by the others; "sheep's tallow is the hue to match it."

This fellow, an under-officer, as I saw by his attire, in spite of his good looks (he had regular features and keen eyes), contrived to assume a most insulting manner. He stopped in front of me, spread his legs wide apart, puffed out his lips, and stared at my hair, cocking his head first upon one side and then upon the other, muttering the while, —

"Tallow! tallow! by every saint in the calendar, or my name is not Otto von Ettergarde! I'll lay you a florin," he cried, addressing one of his companions, "it's nearer to tallow than gold."

I was quite at a loss what to do. To stand there and be further the butt of the German troopers was as far from my liking as it was from my intention, but how to avoid them puzzled me. Retreat into the palace I would not, and yet if I attempted to pass through the courtyard, I felt that they were likely to follow. This last, however, appeared to be my only choice. I had no wish to pick a quarrel with any of them, for fear of incurring Gian Galeazzo's displeasure, so springing swiftly to one side, I had eluded them before they were aware of my intention, and began threading my way between the other groups toward the gateway that led into the piazza. For an instant I thought I had done with them, but erelong I heard several of them hot at my heels.

"Stay, my sweet maid-face!" cried he who had declared himself to be Otto von Ettergarde, breaking out in Italian. "Tarry, my fair candle-locks! By my faith, you are well named, for you run as nimbly as your same stinking tallow in hot weather."

"Assuredly," I said to myself, "this pestilent fellow is growing to be most offensive!" but I still kept to my resolve to pay no heed to him.

He, having evidently determined to see to what lengths he could push me, now overstepped the mark, for he slipped forward, caught my lifted foot in his, and all but tripped me upon my face. In fact, I only saved myself from sprawling at full length upon the stones of the courtyard by clutching hold of a big trooper near at hand who was burnishing his breastplate, causing him to drop this with a great clatter upon the pavement.

"God's wounds!" cried he, drawing back as though he would fetch me a buffet; "what do you mean?"

I saw his good nature in his countenance, and felt sure that I could pacify him; as for the others, I cared not now what I said.

"I crave your pardon most earnestly," I began, "and beg you to believe that I had no intention of making you drop your armor. These insolent fellows," I exclaimed, turning on von Ettergarde and his companions, who stood by, grinning at my discomfiture, "were the cause of the accident. Because, forsooth, I have the misfortune to possess but one suit of clothes, they needs must mock at me, and because the color of my hair is not to their taste, they needs must fleer at me, dog my steps, and try the scurvy trick of tripping me."

All this I said in the troopers' own

tongue, and blank-faced most of them looked on a sudden. As for the big soldier against whom I had been thrown, he immediately espoused my cause.

"Give over, von Ettergarde," said he. "Why do you pester the youngster?"

A malicious look crossed the trooper's handsome features as he saw he was likely to be deprived of his sport.

"What's that to you?" he cried. "I thought Rupert Hartzheim made it his boast that he always minded his own affairs. Hereafter we shall look to find him acting as sponsor for every young popinjay in Pavia."

I was now so thoroughly incensed that I doubt if I should have been able to restrain myself had the whole line of the Visconti, from the original Matteo down, been ranged before me. I strode forward and faced von Ettergarde.

"While I thank Rupert Hartzheim, as you call him, for his kindly interest in me," I said, "I am quite able to stand up for my own rights against such a mannerless knave as you, even though you do wear his Lordship's insignia."

Hartzheim clutched me by the arm, and pulled me away, but von Ettergarde, flushed and fierce, and growing more angry each instant owing to the outcries of those who had gathered about us, rushed at me with drawn blade.

"Softly! softly!" said Hartzheim, interposing his stalwart bulk between us. "You are but getting a repayment in your own coin."

"He called me a mannerless knave!" sputtered my whilom tormentor.

"I spoke only the truth," cried I. "You had best let us have it out," I said to Hartzheim.

"There seems to be no other way," the latter answered, looking from one of us to the other. "But mark you, von Ettergarde," he said sternly, "if you hurt the youngling fatally, you have me to deal with. Choose your second, since it must be so, and let the affair be conducted as quietly as may be. The garden will serve for the place of meeting. The morning is hardly old yet, and her little ladyship will not be abroad. Give back there!" he called to those who were clustering about us.

I saw by the way the troopers respected his authority that he was one of some rank among them, though what I could not discover from his dress. He strode toward the entrance by which I had emerged into the courtyard, and I followed, with von Ettergarde and his second hard after. At the doorway he halted, and bade von Ettergarde and his companion lead on.

"I would speak with the young man," he said, "and I doubt not that you will conduct us to the spot straight enough," this last with a meaning look which told me that my antagonist was no stranger to these encounters.

As we moved along the passage a few paces in the rear of the other two, Hartzheim said, lowering his voice, —

"It is too late now to withdraw, but you had best not endeavor to stand long against him. He is a most expert swordsman. Let him disarm you after you have made a show of resistance, and then I will interfere."

"Would you counsel me to act the coward?" said I.

"I would save you from harm. It is a sin to pit such as you against such as he."

"But I have met my man more than once ere this!"

"That may be, but he was never Otto von Ettergarde."

My mind flew back several months to the time when I had last drawn blade in the duello, and I saw before me the great square of San Petronio in Bologna, and the swaggering bravo whom I had encountered as I strolled back to my lodgings through the moonlight from the rooms of a friend. The lout had been offering some insult to a defenceless wench whose cries arrested my steps. Was I likely, I asked myself, to be harder pressed now than then when I needed all the finesse taught me by the best masters to preserve a whole skin, for my antagonist proved to be one of the most skilful men-at-arms employed by the Bentigvoli?

As I was turning this over in my mind, never for a second thinking to follow Hartzheim's advice, we passed from the dusk of the corridor into a sunny pleasance where there were flowers in bloom, and fruit trees casting plots of cool shade, and at the bottom of which, near to the enclosing wall, stood a vine-embowered summer-house. It was here, as I afterward learned, that Gian Galeazzo's daughter, Valentina, she who was afterward wedded to the Duke of Orleans, came to frolic with her maids. Now to all appearances the place was deserted, save that the birds were making a tremulous little twitter in the boughs.

As we walked down the privet-bordered path toward the summer-house I espied a clove-pink, my favorite flower, growing within reach, so I leaned over and plucked it, and having inhaled two or three whiffs of its fragrance, thrust the stem into one of the eyelets of my doublet. When I looked up from arranging the blossom I was aware that Hartzheim was regarding me curiously.

"By the mass!" said he, "but you are the coolest youngster I ever fell in with." Then he continued to eye me to discover if my action were bravado, but he soon saw that it was not, and so he was quite chirk when we passed to the rear of the summer-house, where we found a swarded open space used by the maids for buffet-ball. There were marks upon the turf which told of the recent presence of heavier feet, and I came to the conclusion that the play here practised was not all of it the innocent amusement of maids.

"Look out for him! he is a devil if you oppose him too long, and he may have no mercy," was Hartzheim's last injunction, and I knew he hoped to prevail upon me to yield to his advice and make the encounter little short of a farce.

That Hartzheim's words were true, and my adversary was a devil, I speedily discovered when our weapons crossed; for there came a deadly gleam, a cruel exultation, into his handsome eyes. Blood-letting was evidently the man's delight, and he thought me but another mouse to be toyed with, and then maimed or crushed at will.   I had never encountered just his like, yet I was in no whit put out.

"Jesu, a pretty counter!" I heard Hartzheim cry, as I turned aside a vicious thrust at my left shoulder, and that was the last of his exclamations I can recall, though I was conscious from time to time that he gave vent to some enthusiastic expression.   How the affair would have ended I cannot say, for we were most evenly matched, had it not been brought to a close by a most unlooked-for interruption.   We were plying at one another with all our energies, every nerve alert, anticipating sudden changes of fence, meeting each subtle attack, when a sharp "hold!" startled us.   A third sword struck ours in air, and between us stood Jacobo del Verme, scowling, fierce, like an avenging fate.   As we started back in amazement, letting the points of our weapons drop simultaneously on the sward, a voice that cut me to the very marrow fell upon my ears from the direction of the summer-house.   As I swung about, I caught the ferret eyes of the Lord of Pavia full upon me.

"Very pretty play, gentlemen, very pretty play, upon my word," said he, and he laughed with a glee which I could not fathom.

I was expecting that he would dismiss me with scathing words for allowing myself to be drawn into a quarrel on the very morning when he had bidden me to another interview with him, but he came forward and clapped me upon the arm.

"Bravo!" he cried. "I am proud to appoint you to the lieutenancy in the palace guard. Von Ettergarde," he continued, "you played your part bravely, and shall not be forgotten. Give your hand to Luigi della Verria."

The German could scarce do otherwise than obey; and though I now realized that the quarrel had been put upon me by previous arrangement, and should have borne the man no ill-will for acting under orders, it was with an inward protest that I took his hand, while in his eyes I read that he would have fallen to sword-play again with far greater liking than to hand-shaking.

In this strange manner was my fitness for a guardsman's office proved.

"A deep one, his Lordship, though he may not look it," said Rupert Hartzheim to me, as we walked side by side out of the pleasance.

Chapter V

My First Outriding

MY duties as lieutenant of the palace guard were not arduous. Most of my orders came directly from Gian Galeazzo himself, rather than from the captain under whose nominal authority I acted. Little by little, as the weeks lapsed, I found myself becoming the confidential messenger of the Lord of Pavia, the one through whom he issued his commands, the one to whom he entrusted various communications.

As if by tacit agreement von Ettergarde and I avoided one another. We were both aware that any renewal of our quarrel would draw upon us the wrath of the Visconti, in whose favor we both desired to sun ourselves, for it began to be patent that there was some unusual undertaking towards. Of Rupert Hartzheim, however, I saw much. He was my senior by fully twenty years, and a kindlier nature God never planted in his great human garden. This good friend taught me horsemanship, in which I was sadly deficient, and instructed me in the use of the lance.

I came in daily contact with the Lord of Pavia, and yet I never seemed to get nearer to him than at first. His was an inscrutable mind. Strive as I would to grasp his motives, I was ever eluded. Now he would appear immersed in charities, in the talk of the schools, and the next time I encountered him he would be in close consultation with Del Verme over some matter that I knew had to do with things military. I soon discovered, too, that he kept a keen watch over the condition of affairs in neighboring principalities. He had agents in Milan, in Mantua, in Verona. His treatment of me was in every respect gracious. He went so far as to interest himself in attempting to bring about a reconciliation between my father and myself, in which, however, he was far from successful, my enraged parent assuring him that he was glad to be rid of a son who deported himself with such obstinacy and ingratitude.

One morning, a month after my meeting with von Ettergarde, I was summoned into Gian Galeazzo's presence. I found him in the small closet where he had received me the night I had first visited the palace, and, as on the previous occasion, Del Verme was with him.

When I appeared he scarcely gave me time to make my greetings, but broached the subject he had in his thought at once.

" I have not been disappointed in you, Della Verria," he said, "and I am now going to try you further in an affair where you will be obliged to use your head as well as your hands. If you carry this through creditably, and Del Verme agrees with me that you will, I shall store it up in my remembrance as a debt to be one day balanced. What you are to do is this. In the employ of the Marquis of Mantua is a captain named Gerino Ardotti. This soldier I wish to enlist under my banner. You are to seek him out wherever he may be. Should you find he is not in Mantua, discover whither he has gone, follow him, and submit to him my proposal; namely, that if he will join my company, his pay shall be five florins per month more than whatever he may now be receiving. Indeed, I would double that offer rather than not secure his services. In conducting this negotiation your adroitness will be put to a test, for you have a grasping old war-dog to deal with. I would impress upon you the necessity of the greatest caution should you by any chance be questioned in regard to affairs here at Pavia. See that you sustain my reputa-tion, which is that of a man devoted to studies, reforms, and charities. Bear in mind, too, that it is often convenient to have the plea of ignorance ready if an awkward query be put to you. Now go. Del Verme will tell you that a trusty messenger is one who rides in haste."

I saluted the two men gravely, and strode toward the door.

"One moment," said his Lordship. "The horse you have been recently using is from this time yours. I would that you should go well mounted."

My delight showed upon my face. Hawkwood, as I had christened the fine bay I had been riding, from my admiration of the noted English captain, was a splendid animal, one which any soldier might be proud to possess.

"You are most gracious!" I exclaimed. "Neither horse nor rider shall fail you."

Within half an hour I was in the saddle. As I passed through the piazza I encountered von Ettergarde, and could not resist casting upon him a scornful and exultant look. I had a feeling that he followed my progress through the square with jealous and resentful eyes, and enjoyed what I considered to be my triumph. Such is ever the foolish spirit of youth.

I cannot recall that any ride taken in after years afforded me quite the fine pleasure that did this first day's outgoing upon my quest. Was I not the trusted messenger of a great lord,—one who, though not thus looked upon by his neighbors, was in reality great, or at least so I told myself? Had I not a spirited animal beneath me, one that obeyed every turn of the rein, and responded to every pressure of the knee? For the time being I wholly forgot my family troubles, and lost myself in the sunshine, in the enjoyment of the fresh green of growing things, and in dreams of the career that seemed to be so auspiciously opening before me.

I slept that night at Cremona, and late the afternoon of the following day rode through the landward gate of Mantua, which is over against the former city. Having sought out a quiet inn and seen to Hawkwood's comfort, I hastened to remove the dust from my garments; and

then, after having refreshed myself with a
bottle of wine and a small pasty, inquired
the way to the house of a friend whom I
had known at the University. By good
fortune he was within and gave me a most
cordial welcome, insisting that I bring my
few belongings from the public house and
bide for the night beneath his father's
roof. This I was pleased to do, after
having charged the innkeeper that my
steed have the best of care.

As my master had not given me the
address of his Mantuan agent, I concluded that it was his desire that I should
not enter into communication with him,
and resolved to ascertain through my
friend if the man who was the object of
my journey were in the city, and provided
he were, where he might that evening be
found. I did not wish, if I could avoid
it, to seek him personally at the palace of
the Marquis.

I revealed to my former University
comrade no more than suited my purpose
in regard to my change of fortune. He,
however, not knowing my father's senti-

ments, was in no way surprised that I had abandoned jurisprudence for the profession of arms; and, since I had, he appeared to take it as perfectly natural that I should have a mission with Gerino Ardotti, whom he knew as a captain of note, and whose whereabouts he readily agreed to ascertain. It was doubtless fortunate for me that my friend was neither inquisitive nor suspicious, else he might have wondered what I, confessedly in the service of the Lord of Pavia, could have for the ear of one of the officers of Francesco da Gonzaga.

Dinner over, my friend left me to the tender mercies of his father, a wealthy burgher whose soul was wrapt up in his mercantile ventures, while he sallied out to do my errand. I was beginning to be consumed with ennui at the discourse of the worthy Mantuan when my friend returned, and bore me off with him to a promenade on the Lago di Mezzo.

"Your warrior is abroad on business for the Marquis," said he, as we emerged into the street. "I learned the fact from

one of my acquaintances among the soldiers at the Castello. The man was sure
he had gone to Brescia, and might not
return for a number of days."

"To Brescia!" said I, with no little
disappointment in my tone, for I had
hoped to find Ardotti without further
search.

"Yes," answered my friend; "but why
should you be down-hearted? You know
that it will give me the greatest pleasure
to have you with me until the captain
returns. I think I can promise you that
the time will not be dull."

My mind reverted, I acknowledge it
to my shame, to my late conversation with
my comrade's father. That assuredly had
not been exciting.

"You know," I said, "how pleased I
should be to tarry with you, but unfortu-
nately my orders are imperative. I must
be off on the track of Messer Ardotti
on the morrow. Your informant did not
by any chance let fall where the worthy
captain is likely to be found in Brescia?"

"Ah, but he did! At the house of

Vincenzo Canaro. That, it seems, is why the bold man of war is likely to linger. His host keeps a generous larder, and the Signor Capitano loves a stuffed capon better than he loves a quarrel."

"Canaro! Canaro!" I repeated. The name sounded familiar, and yet I could not for the instant recall in what connection I had heard it.

"Yes," returned my friend. "This was one of the richest and most powerful families in Brescia before the Brusati, whose allies they were, were dispossessed of the lordship of the city by the Visconti. Vincenzo is the last male descendant of the house."

What mission can Ardotti, a captain in the employ of the Marquis of Mantua, have with the last of the house of Canaro who owes allegiance to Bernabo Visconti, Lord of Milan? thought I. It was evident that some sort of an intrigue was on foot, whether for good or ill I was unable to conjecture, though it seemed likely the former, since I had come to regard any combination which tended toward the defeat of the schemes of the detestable uncle of my master not only righteous but just.

I fear my friend found me but a stupid companion that evening, for his information had started a distracting train of queries in my mind, and made me indifferent to the gayeties of Mantua's most fashionable promenade.

I was up betimes the next morning, on the plea of haste, and was bidding my friend adieu at the door of the inn whither he had accompanied me just as the good folk of the city were beginning to stir abroad.

When I passed into Brescia there were yet fully three hours of the afternoon remaining, and I resolved to seek out the residence of Vincenzo Canaro without delay. As I progressed toward the centre of the town, I began to see indications of a great bustle in the streets. Houses and shops were decorated with gay streamers, and on inquiring the reason for the stir and the display I learned that it was the fête-day of our Lady of Brescia. When

I came to seek for accommodations for myself and Hawkwood, I discovered, to my chagrin, that the best inns were filled to overflowing, and it was only after a protracted search that I hit upon a little hostelry just off the Piazza Vecchia, where, for an exorbitant sum, I secured for myself a tiny room high up under the roof, and for my steed a dark corner in an ill-kept stable. It was useless to grumble, so I determined to make the best of the situation.

I had descended the stairs, and was about entering the street, not choosing to inquire the whereabouts of the Canaro house at the inn, when I encountered the landlord, a suave, obsequious person, abnormally spare, with hands that made me think of a hawk's talons. He had just come from the small wine-room, which I saw was crowded with customers. He renewed his regrets that he was not able to see me better bestowed, and asked if there were anything further he could do which would add to my comfort. I assured him that there was nothing, and started to pass on, when he a second time arrested my steps, in this instance with a request that I try his wine, which he boasted to be from a choice vintage. Thirsty from my long ride, and telling myself that it was always well to be on good terms with "mine host," I assented, and followed him into the room from which he had emerged. The company, though oddly assorted, was perfectly orderly. Most of the men were seated upon rude benches about rough tables, though a few were leaning against the smoke-blackened walls. There chanced to be a vacant place at a small table in one corner, and this the landlord pressed me to take.

"These gentlemen will not mind, I'm sure," he said, addressing two men who were here seated, looking indifferently about them, keeping constantly a tight grip upon two huge beakers as though they feared these objects, unless thus restrained, might take unto themselves legs and walk away. They assented civilly enough, and the landlord left to go himself in pursuit of the wine, his assistants being occupied.

That the two men at the table were not civilians I saw at a glance, although this was what their dress, with the exception of their swords, would have led one to infer. Both had hard, shrewd, unscrupulous faces, and I noticed their hands as they clasped their drinking-cups were large and muscular.

"You have had a long ride," said one of them, as I leaned back and stretched my limbs, endeavoring to find an easy position, for the bench was anything but a comfortable seat. "I noticed your horse as you halted at the door."

"Yes, something of a ride," I replied, not liking the manner of the men.

"So had we but yesterday," the other remarked.

" Perhaps the young Signore is, like us, a stranger at the fête of our Lady of Brescia ? " said the first speaker.

Both looked at me questioningly, and I was compelled to confess that I was.

" Doubtless you have a similar gala

" For some reason these three men were endeavoring to
draw me out." — Page 63

day at your home in honor of some patron saint," the other said.

To this observation I did not feel compelled to reply, as I saw the landlord approaching with my draught. When he had set it before me, instead of retiring, he stood by and joined in the conversation, which took a turn that very speedily aroused my suspicions. For some reason these three men, the landlord and the two who had declared themselves to be strangers in Brescia, were endeavoring to draw me out, — to discover from whence I came. I had been cautious in my replies before I arrived at this conclusion, but I was doubly so afterward, and I flatter myself for one unschooled in the art of evasion I acquitted myself well. Finally, having finished my wine, I bade the two men a polite " good day," and without any undue haste, glad though I was to be out of their company, sought the street.

Chapter VI

In a Brescia Garden

ONCE out of sight of the inn, I lost no time in quickening my pace, and was soon mingling with the gay crowd that thronged the Piazza Vecchia. I had a feeling that I might be followed, though why any one should wish to dog my footsteps I could not conjecture. My recent experience was an enigma to me. Had I stumbled into a den of cutpurses where the landlord was in league with the plunderers, or were these men of the inn the political agents of Bernabo Visconti, watchful in his interest, and on the lookout for messengers from some rival lord to those in Brescia who might be conspiring against the Milan tyrant? The latter was by far the more

likely solution to the riddle, and I determined if I found Ardotti, whether I was
successful in bringing to pass my master's
wishes or not, I would relate to him my
experience. He might be able to shed
some light upon the matter.

Under most circumstances I should
have taken a hearty pleasure in the pictu-
resque scene which the piazza presented.
At one end of the square a party of mum-
mers were acting, in a sort of dumb show,
various scenes from the life of the blessed
lady in whose memory the fête was given.
The booths of the confetti-sellers were
plentifully dotted about, and masquers
and buffoons were at their mad pranks
wherever the throng was densest. There
was an infinite variety of costume, and no
garb, however eccentric, appeared to attract special notice.

As I threaded my way through this
motley gathering, I began to wonder to
whom I had best apply for information in
regard to the location of the house of
Vincenzo Canaro. After reflecting for a
little, it occurred to me that probably any

of the larger tradesmen would be able to tell me what I wished to know, and I directed my steps toward that side of the square where the more imposing shops were situated. I had just made up my mind to enter one, that of a fruiterer and general provision merchant, when, on turning to glance about me, I found myself face to face with the two men of the inn.

"Ah, we meet again!" cried one of them, with an attempt at affability. "A gay sight, is it not?" and he waved his hand toward the human mass now pushing excitedly toward a tumbler who was giving an exhibition of his skill in the centre of the piazza.

Perturbed and annoyed as I was by this encounter, I restrained my inclination to answer rudely, and made reply that I found it most interesting. With that I sauntered on, wondering if it were to be my fate to encounter these individuals at every turn. I had no further doubt in regard to the profession of the men. They were bravos. They could not conceal their swaggering martial carriage under the garb of men of peace.

Noting a thoroughfare of considerable width from which quite a stream of pleasurers was debouching into the square, I made my way toward it, not venturing to glance behind me until I had reached the corner. My single look revealed to me no sign that I had been followed, and not thinking it advisable to seem suspicious and watchful in case I had been, without hesitation I plunged into the stream of passers, won through them, and entered the first door I came to, that of a little shop which proved to be the stall of a bookseller. I could not have been more fortunate, for when I mentioned the name of Vincenzo Canaro, the proprietor's wizened face lighted up with evident pleasure.

"The Signore is a most excellent customer of mine," he said. "His house? certainly! It is quite near." Then he proceeded to give me careful instructions as to how I might most quickly reach it. In five minutes I was at the door.

The palace — for palace it was — at that time occupied by the last of the Canari, was situated in a quiet street where the noise of the fête penetrated but faintly. While I stood contemplating the family arms above the entrance, the porter appeared.

" Is the Captain Gerino Ardotti stopping here ? " I asked.

" He is," was the answer.

" May I see him for a few moments ? Say to him, that I come from a distance, on a mission of much importance."

" I will inquire if the captain will see you. Step within."

Before I had passed into the courtyard I cast my eyes up and down the street. No one was standing near, but in the distance, at the corner of a crossing thoroughfare, several loiterers were visible. It was impossible, however, to say if the men of the inn were of the number.

In a large reception-room on the second floor of the palace I awaited the return of the servant. I was not kept long, for presently he appeared, saying that the captain would be with me at once. Hardly had he delivered his message when there were heavy steps without, and a man of florid countenance and well-rounded build entered the room. From what I had heard of him at Mantua I judged Ardotti to be one of self-indulgent disposition, a lover of the good things of life, and his appearance told me I was not mistaken. Yet back of his jovial air and love of ease there was, as I was presently to discover, a vast deal of shrewdness and much real feeling. I arrived at an agreement with him more readily than I anticipated; still, on the whole, he acted in accordance with the grasping reputation my master had given him.

" I must look out for myself," he said. " If I do not, who will? Now I have no fault to find with my present employer, save that he is afraid of using his money. I believe I have served him well, and am persuaded that he would tell you as much should you ask him. But why am I bound to continue in his service when I can materially better myself elsewhere? I shall, of course, endeavor, to the best of my ability, to execute his present commission ; that accomplished, I am at your master's disposal, and I can promise him that I will be as faithful to him as I have been to the Marquis of Mantua until " — here he paused and looked at me shrewdly — "some one values my sword more highly than he."

All this was said after we had come to an understanding, and I liked Ardotti the better for his perfect frankness.

His attitude was that of many soldiers of fortune. In a time of tranquillity he was perfectly willing to transfer his allegiance from one lord to another, provided he could advance his interests by so doing. If, however, there had been open hostility between Gian Galeazzo and the house of Gonzaga, Ardotti would have been the last man in the world to listen to such a proposal as I had made.

" How is it," said Ardotti suddenly, as though it were an afterthought with him, " that my Lord of Pavia is so anxious to add another captain to his retainers ? His reputation is that of a man of peace and piety, and then he has Del Verme, has he not?"

"Yes, he has Del Verme," I answered; "but it would seem that even as a man of peace he must have some need of at least one other, else had I not been told to seek out Gerino Ardotti wherever he might be."

The soldier smiled at my evasion, and the implied compliment.

"The Visconti of Pavia has an uncle who is not only cruel, but ambitious,— ambitious, it is rumored, to extend his power," said he, casting a swift look at me.

"Is it so?" said I, with seeming surprise and interest; for, although I was perfectly sure of my man, we were not talking together in Pavia, and I had kept constantly in mind my master's advice in regard to caution. "I am but recently come from my studies at Bologna, and there these rumors you speak of do not come to one's ears."

Ardotti took no offence at my second evasion, but cried, as he chuckled a little,—

"There must be some clever teachers of discretion at Bologna!"

"And there are doubtless those at Pavia," said I, rising, "who will speak more frankly than I have done."

"Stay!" exclaimed he, "where are you lodging? The city is so full of folk come to the fête that I am surprised if you have found a place to lay your head."

"I am at the Two Falcons. The other inns were full."

As I said this, it came to me that here was my opportunity to relate to him my experience on my arrival, but he cut in, before I could begin, with,—

"Diavolo! I know the place! The landlord is a grasping wretch, and he keeps a most pestilent cook."

Then a sudden idea seemed to strike him.

"Sit down, sit down again!" he exclaimed, and out of the room he went with all the impetuosity of his sanguine temperament, leaving me in a state bordering upon amazement. I could get no clew in regard to what his extraordinary behavior might mean, and was still trying to find one, when I heard his heavy tread upon the stairs. Presently he came puffing in.

"Signor Canaro, my host, hopes you will tarry and dine with us," he said. Then, in explanation, "I could not let you go back to a vile dinner at that wretched inn."

"It is most kind of Signor Canaro, and of you," I answered. "I shall be delighted to stay if my travel-stained garb will be pardoned."

"You won't think so much about your trunks and your doublet after you have ridden twenty-five years to the wars," laughed he. "Signor Canaro won't mind, and if"—here he broke off. "Come!" he continued, moving toward the door. "He is awaiting us in the garden."

As I followed Ardotti, a trifle surprised at the perfect freedom he seemed to feel in the stately house, I began to wonder what manner of man I was about to meet. He must be of a careless, jovial type, I told myself, in explanation of the apparent intimacy between him and the captain.   There was little time for this sort of conjecture, however ; for, after reaching the palace courtyard, a few steps brought us to a short passage beyond which lay a small but perfectly kept bower of greenery.   As we emerged into this enclosure my conductor started as if surprised, and for an instant seemed about to stop. Then he went on.

"Madonna !" I heard him mutter under his breath, "the Signorina !"

Where one of the paths expanded at the centre of the garden I caught the flutter of a woman's garment.   Thither the captain led me.   We found the last male scion of the house of Canaro seated upon a rustic bench, a book open upon his knee, and near him a girl whose flower-like beauty impressed me strangely the moment I looked upon her.   I was presented in turn to father and daughter. Vincenzo Canaro was past middle life, a slender man with a face in which refinement was the dominant characteristic.   I fancied I detected a certain hesitancy

The Signorina Angela Canaro. — Page 75

about his eyes, although the lower part of his countenance showed considerable force. The expression of his mouth when he spoke was winning in the extreme, and his whole air was that of courtesy and fine breeding. He was in every respect Ardotti's opposite, and I marvelled what the two could have in common.

I fear should I attempt fully to describe Angela Canaro as she appeared to me that day I should be led into hyperbole, a danger by no means common with me. She impressed me as maiden never had done before, and I had seen many both in Pavia and Bologna. What it was about her that appealed to me most it would be difficult to say. She was one of those persons whose charm lay not in one or two attractive features, — the voice, the eyes, — but in the atmosphere which radiated from her whole personality. When she moved I could but think of the grace of the swaying osier; when she laughed it was like — but stay! my pen is already playing pranks with me.

"My friend, the captain, tells me you are a Pavian," said Signor Canaro, after we had exchanged greetings, and were all seated. "I think I must know your father by repute. Has he not written upon jurisprudence?"

I answered that he had.

"You, I judge, are not inclined to follow his example, in the matter of a profession," said the Brescian, smilingly. "Well, we must have upholders of law as well as law-makers."

The conversation for a time was general, and I shortly learned that Signorina Canaro had but that afternoon returned from a visit to some of her kinsfolk in Verona, which accounted for Ardotti's start of surprise on beholding her. After a little, one of the reasons for the friendliness between the captain and his host was explained. Near where Signor Canaro was seated I saw a small table upon which some chessmen lay as though a game had recently been in progress. This led me to remark that my father was an enthusiastic chess-player.

"Doubtless the captain and I would find in him a worthy foe," said Signor Canaro. "We are very fierce enemies ourselves — that is, at chess. If the captain is as shrewd on the battle-field as he is at the chess-board, he is a clever strategist who outwits him. We had just finished a game when you called."

Soon they fell to discussing a certain point of play with great vehemence, and I was left to address my entire conversation to the Signorina, whereat I was nothing loath. She had such a frank, unaffected, and winning way that I found myself, before I was aware of it, confiding to her my hopes and my ambitions. Something in her dark eyes — ah! what eyes they were! — told me that she was interested, and there are few men, I care not who they may be, that can resist when beauty bids them speak about themselves. She, on her part, revealed to me but little of her life, yet there was one thing which she could not conceal, and this was her innate loveliness of character. I seemed to look into her mind and see only what was fair

and pure.   One thing about her surprised
me.   It was a fleeting sadness which at
times crossed her face, a look that had in
it something like fear.   By the time dinner was announced we were upon quite
a friendly footing, and it was not until
toward the close of the meal that anything
occurred to mar an experience which to me
had in it both the reality and unreality of
a dream.   Something that I myself inadvertently said caused the cloud to gather.
The talk had been upon the fête, and the
number of persons attracted thereby to the
city.   This led me to say, —

"I trust all strangers do not arouse the
same suspicion and curiosity which I seem
to excite."

"How so?" said Ardotti quickly.

Thereupon I began relating my experience at the inn.   As I proceeded, I saw
that Ardotti was listening with an intentness of manner I had not marked in him
before.   Signor Canaro leaned back, one
hand upon the arm of his chair, the other
clutching his wine-glass.   On the face of
the Signorina was the look I had already

beheld with wonder, now fixed and inten-
sified. What did it all mean? I tried
to appear not to notice the change which
had come over the three, and continued
with my narration. When I had finished,
Ardotti said, —

" And the men ; tell us more fully what
they were like."

I described them as clearly as I could.

" You think they did not follow you
here ? "

" I cannot be absolutely sure, but I believe not."

No more was said upon the matter, but
after that a decided constraint fell upon
us. As we were walking back to the garden, Ardotti left us, and I saw him hurrying toward the entrance into the street.
He speedily joined us again, however, and
as he did so he exchanged a grave nod
with Signor Canaro.

As soon as was consistent with courtesy
I rose to make my adieus, for I felt that
my presence was an embarrassment to
both father and daughter. Whatever
trouble or danger my story had revealed

to them as being imminent could better be met alone than with a stranger present. However, Ardotti stopped me.

"If you will wait until it grows a trifle darker," he said, "I will go a part of the way to your inn with you."

It was then dusk, and as soon as the stars began to spangle the sky the captain went for his cloak and sword.

"We will try the laneway," he remarked to Signor Canaro.

"I feel that we owe you an apology," said that gentleman, as he offered me his hand, "for our perturbation and exhibition of anxiety. I trust that you may one day give us the pleasure of seeing you in Brescia again, for I assure you we are not in the habit of thus disturbing our guests."

I expressed my pleasure at his invitation, and my regret that I should have been the one to cause the distress of mind which he and his daughter were experiencing. To Angela Canaro I said, as I bade her farewell, —

"While I know, Signorina, that you

have two valiant protectors in your father and Captain Ardotti, should the time ever come when you need a third, I beg you to believe that my sword is entirely at your service."

"Oh, thank you, Signore," she cried, "though I pray Heaven there may never be such a dire necessity."

So I went out into the dark laneway with Ardotti, dreaming that her eyes had said to me more than her lips, as I caught her parting look in the spring starlight.

G

Chapter VII

A Night at the Two Falcons

"THE street in front of the palace is watched," said Ardotti, as we entered the lane.

"I fancied as much," I answered.

"Doubtless you are puzzling over the why and wherefore of all this," he went on. "I have accompanied you that I may explain the situation at least in part, for an explanation and warning are due you, since by entering the house of Vincenzo Canaro you have made yourself an object of suspicion, and I believe are likely to be assaulted at any moment as long as you remain in Brescia."

He led the way rapidly, turning abruptly into another lane before we had gone far.

"There is a little wine-house here," he said, "where we can talk and not be molested."

Presently we came to a small building whose lower windows showed a glimmer of light. Ardotti entered without hesitation. There was no one within save the proprietor, who greeted us with marked respect.

"A room, Bruno, and some wine, and see that we are not disturbed!" exclaimed Ardotti.

"There is no danger that the Signori will be disturbed," was the reply. "The whole city is viewing the illumination in the piazza."

"I shall not keep you long," said Ardotti when we were seated with a flagon of the wine of Asti before us, "for you had best be back at your inn as soon as may be, and I at the palace. Though you did not see fit to trust me this afternoon, for which I do not in the least blame you, I am going to trust you now, since something tells me that you are worthy of being trusted, and a time may perhaps come when the information which I am about to give you will enable you to aid those whom I am trying to assist. Now do you follow me closely, for I shall not waste words. When the Brusati were deposed from the overlordship of Brescia by the Visconti, the Canari fell with them, and lost a greater part of their possessions. Latterly, however, they prospered, and Vincenzo's inheritance was princely. Bernabo Visconti has, for a number of years, been scheming to get this wealth into his hands. He dare not seize it openly, that would be too gross a piece of injustice to be practised even by a tyrant such as he, but he has conceived a plan of marrying one of his sons to Signorina Canaro, and thus obtaining his wish. I scarcely need tell you how his proposals have been met both by father and daughter. Bernabo, however, will not be put off. He is constant in his importuning, and Signor Canaro fears that he may finally resort to force. Hearing by chance a few months since how matters stood, the Marquis of Mantua, formerly a friend of Signor Canaro, despatched me to Brescia to try to arrange an alliance between the Signorina and his nephew, and thus frustrate the schemes of the Lord of Milan. Being a Brescian by birth, and my father having been in the employ of the house of Canaro in its more favored days, I was received as a friend, and all seemed to be progressing happily, when something displeasing came to my lady's ears in regard to my master's nephew. This caused a hitch in the negotiations. I am now on my third visit to Brescia, and still no definite decision has been reached. Signor Canaro is favorably inclined toward the proposal of the Marquis, yet he fears to accept, even should his daughter overcome her compunctions, lest Bernabo declare all his possessions forfeited. The story of your experience confirmed me in what I had already suspected — that through unknown and treacherous means Bernabo has ascertained that some sort of negotiations are in progress between the Marquis and Signor Canaro, and that he intends to discover what they are and

thwart them.   Several times since my
arrival I have fancied I was spied upon.
It will be no easy matter for me to get
back to Mantua with a whole skin, for I
doubt not Bernabo's hirelings — and there
are more than the two you encountered
— have orders to find out at all hazards
what is going on."

"Have you not then risked the safety
of the Signorina and her father by telling
me?" said I.

"No," he replied, "for I feel sure I
have not misjudged you; and now let me
show you your own danger.   Chance led
you to the Two Falcons, and your late
arrival indicated to the watchful agents of
Bernabo that you had no special interest
in the fête.   Your horse gave signs of
having been ridden far, and on being
questioned you carefully avoided revealing whence you came.   You aroused suspicion, and I feel positive that you were
followed to the Canaro palace.   In the
minds of those entrusted with this affair
you are connected with the Marquis of
Mantua, and are doubtless put down as

being an emissary from him either to Signor Canaro or to me. It will be thought that you are returning with some sort of a message, either written or verbal. I am positive that an attempt will be made to discover what that message is, and those interested will pause at nothing. Had I not revealed to you the real situation, your danger would still have been the same; for had you been captured you would not have been able to convince your captors of your ignorance. Now that you know the truth you will act with greater energy and caution."

" I shall certainly not betray your confidence."

" I knew you would not."

" What would you advise me to do ? "

" Barricade your door to-night, and get off, if you can manage it, before any one is stirring in the morning. Once outside the city, spare neither whip nor spur."

" Do you see no way out of this terrible dilemma for Signor Canaro and his daughter ? " said I, the image of the lovely Signorina in all her distress and beauty rising appealingly before me.

Ardotti shook his head.

"Should they accept the proposal of the Marquis now, I fear it would avail little. They have hesitated too long. I doubt not that the agents of Bernabo would forcibly interfere should Signor Canaro and his daughter attempt to leave Brescia."

"But the Signorina has just been in Verona. Why did she not remain? Her father might have joined her there."

"And might not. It is highly probable that an accident would have happened to him on the way. The case, I fear, is hopeless unless —" Ardotti paused.

"Unless?" cried I, eagerly.

"Unless they can temporize, and, in the meanwhile, something occurs to divert the attention of Bernabo. Did you not think I was remarkably willing to enter the service of your master? No? Well, it would not do to seem too eager; there was really a reason other than personal advantage. I would do anything to help Signor Canaro and the Signorina, and the moment I heard your proposal it flashed upon me that there was something back of it.   Here, I said to myself, is perhaps the chance.   Jacopo del Verme is in command at Pavia.   Where he is there is likely to be shrewd counsel and decisive movement.   Against whom would that movement be unless against Bernabo, who, it is known, has designs upon his nephew's possessions?"

"You reason well," said I.

"I have had my eyes and ears open," said he.   "But come, we must tarry here no longer.   I will show you the most desirable route to the Two Falcons, one which will enable you to avoid the piazza. Then we must part, but I hope within a week that you will see me in Pavia.   That is my message to Gian Galeazzo."

We went quickly out into the night. Ardotti guided me through several streets, and then pointed out to me how to continue on my way.

"May good luck go with you," he said, gripping my hand.   "Be watchful, and do not cease to be bold."

Soon the darkness swallowed him, and I was hurrying toward the inn. Did Ardotti himself love Angela Canaro? Was this the explanation of his eagerness to aid father and daughter? Clearly something beyond his desire faithfully to serve the Marquis of Mantua actuated him. Though at first I had not been especially attracted toward this blunt and jovial soldier, it would have caused me genuine regret had I known I was never to set eyes upon him again, and that in less than a week's time he would lie in a nameless grave, foully done to death by the hirelings of Bernabo Visconti.

I succeeded in slipping past the inn and reaching the stable unobserved. As I stood in the background, waiting for an opportunity to get a word with the hostler who was saddling the horses of three boisterous fellows from Renato, it occurred to me that it might be well to attempt leaving Brescia that night. The uncertainty of the situation was not without its effect on me, and I longed to be beyond the walls, upon Hawkwood's back. Then, even though I might go astray in the darkness, I should feel safe and free, but here, not knowing what man might prove to be a spy, there could be no sense of security, even though I slept behind bolted doors.

Finally the three comrades rode noisily away. I slipped a gold florin from my pocket and approached the hostler. His manner was not encouraging, but I was not deterred thereby. I twirled the coin between my thumb and forefinger, and as it gave back the dull light of the lantern I saw a gleam come into the man's eyes, and a gradual relaxing of his furrowed brow. A bit of gold like that was something more rare to him than was a brimming casket of the same yellow discs to the rich merchant or lord.

"You may saddle my horse," I said, as the man's fingers closed convulsively upon the coin. "I may wish to leave to-night. Do you know how long the city gates will be open?"

"Till midnight, Signore, but"—he paused and looked about him as though the shadows might conceal a listener, then drawing a step nearer and dropping his voice, he continued — " would it not be better to wait till early morning — five o'clock, say ? The horse will be ready then, and the door of the stable unfastened. I shall sleep in the loft on the hay to-night, for there is no room within ; just at the head of these stairs, Signore," and he pointed to a dark corner where I could dimly distinguish a flight of steps leading upward.

I looked at the man several seconds without speaking.

" You see, Signore," he said still in an undertone, " there are likely to be few folk abroad at five in the morning."

" But the city gates ? "

" The Signore could rouse the gate-keeper."

" And the inn ? "

" The Signore will not find the fastenings of the outer door difficult to undo, and it is a time when most people sleep soundly."

I saw the fellow was advising me honestly and wisely. He had said enough to tell me that an attempt to leave Brescia that night would be fraught with danger. His manner in itself was a warning. No doubt the two approaches to the inn were watched, and while I might slip by on foot unnoticed, as I had already done, such a thing would be impossible on horseback.

I did not think it desirable to press the hostler for more information than he had volunteered. I had no wish to get him into trouble, and what I had already learned was quite sufficient to lead me to a decision.

"I will take your advice," I said, "and if it prove good, you shall not be forgotten."

"May the Virgin guard the Signore!" cried the man.

As I passed through the doorway of the inn I encountered the landlord.

"You did not dine with us," he said. "I can assure you that you missed a good dinner. No host in Brescia stocked his cellar for the fête more carefully than I."

"I should have done justice to your

good things had I been here," I answered.
" My appetite is not something I leave at
home.   It travels with me."

" By the by," said he, " I can give you
better quarters on the morrow."

" Thank you," I replied, " we will talk
about that in the morning.   Now I am
off to bed, for I am more than weary."

I mounted the two flights of narrow
stairs, and made my way to the cramped,
low-ceilinged nook where I was to sleep.
I had paid my night's reckoning when I
took the room (this the host said was his
rule on fête days), so if I succeeded in
carrying out the hostler's suggestion I
should leave no unsatisfied debt behind
me.   There was but a flimsy fastening upon the door, so not until I had
dragged the iron bedstead against it, did I
feel secure against intrusion from that
quarter.   I now threw open the single
window, through which the lately risen
moon was shining, and looked out.
Twenty feet below was the almost flat
roof of an extension — doubtless the
kitchen.   It did not occur to me that I

had anything to fear from this direction, so I left the window, which swung backward, ajar, the air being unbearably close, extinguished the candle, and stretched myself out upon the bed, removing from my person nothing save my sword, which I placed at my side.   The possibility that I might oversleep gave me no anxiety.   Since entering the service of Gian Galeazzo I had become accustomed to early rising, and I was confident that I should wake at the peep of day.   What I feared was that I should get little or no rest at all, so excited was my brain with the happenings which had been crowded into the last few hours.

As I lay, with wide eyes, upon the hard mattress, my thoughts hovered about Angela Canaro, and however I tried to will otherwise, they would revert to her. More than once had I fancied myself heart-touched before, but what I now experienced was far different from any sensation I had previously known. Not only was my admiration kindled by her beauty, but my sympathies were moved, and all the chivalry in my nature stirred by the trying position in which she was placed. Yet what could I, who had practically renounced my family and my inheritance and was now but a poor man-at-arms, do to aid the unfortunate maiden? I felt willing to dare anything, but my brain evolved no plan, and so hour after hour I groped blankly. Where a soldier of the shrewdness of Gerino Ardotti could see no light was it likely that any would come to me, I asked myself.

The moon-rays shifted and flooded the room, but gradually through sheer brain-exhaustion I grew drowsy, and became unconscious. I had a dream of being strangled, and awoke with a start to find there was a hand upon my throat and a knee upon my chest.

"Your message," said a voice which I was sure I had heard before; "produce it if it is written, tell it if it is not, or I will throttle your life out of you."

The room had grown shadowy, but I could see a pair of fierce eyes burning down upon me from behind a black mask.

I gasped and struggled, but the grip upon my throat tightened until my head swam.

"Yes," I contrived to ejaculate.

My throat was loosened, but the oppressive weight was still heavy on my chest.

"In my doublet," said I. "I will give it to you."

The knee was lifted, and, as the man partly straightened himself, I realized that but one of his feet was upon the floor. With a desperate twist and squirm I gathered myself and leaped at him, clasping him about the middle, digging my head and shoulders into his stomach. So wholly unexpected was this assault that he lost his balance, toppled over backward, and down I came on top of him with my full weight. His head struck violently upon the boards, and my shoulder completely knocked the wind out of him, so, while I scrambled to my feet, there he lay like a collapsed bladder inflated by some child and crushed by an inadvertent foot. To add to the noise, my sword fell with a great clatter. I stooped and tore the mask from his face. It was one of the two bravos of the inn. While I was bending over him the room was suddenly darkened. I turned toward the window, and beheld a man about to throw one leg over the sill. There was no time to seize a weapon, so I sprang at him with outstretched arms. With all my force I threw myself against him. His grip upon the casing was but slight, and though he had a dagger in his disengaged hand, I was upon him ere he had a chance to use it. His body seemed to poise a moment in air before he lost all support; he clutched wildly at the ladder by which he and his companion had gained the room, then his cry of mingled rage and despair rang out on the night as he plunged sidewise downward upon the furrowed tiles of the extension. His motionless form held me for a moment spell-bound, then I recollected my first antagonist and turned quickly to him. He was beginning to recover consciousness, so I hurriedly fastened his hands and feet with strips of the bed-linen, lest he should attempt further mischief, caught up my sword, and began nimbly to descend the ladder. I fancied the landlord was somewhere about, and before venturing to drop from the roof of the extension I tried to penetrate the dark corners of the enclosure below, thinking perhaps I might discover him. I did not catch sight of him, however, and soon I was on the ground, speeding swiftly toward the door of the stable. Rushing in, I roused the hostler.

"Quick!" I cried, as he descended from the loft; "my horse!"

Without a question he began hastily to saddle Hawkwood. While this was going forward I kept watch of the rear door of the inn. Presently I saw the landlord and a burly tapster steal out and peer about. With my sword drawn I sprang toward them.

"Back!" I exclaimed, "or it will go ill with you."

The landlord retreated, but the tapster held his ground. He had a heavy blade with which he cut at me viciously, but he lacked agility, and when I had slashed his shoulder he ran howling within.

By this time Hawkwood stood ready in the stable door, and with a feeling of relief and exultation I sprang to the saddle. The hostler was waiting silently and expectantly.

"Here," said I, giving him two florins, whereat he blessed me devoutly, "you can do me one more good turn."

"The Signore has but to name it."

"Show me the nearest way to the southern gate, to the Porta Cremona."

He put his hand upon the pommel and ran alongside.

"I will say that the Signore's sword persuaded me to this if I am ever questioned."

"I would that you had a horse to ride with me," said I. "I could promise you pleasanter employment than you have at the inn of the Two Falcons."

"I would follow the Signore, — may the saints attend him! — but there is the wife and little one."

At length he released his hold on the pommel.

"The way is straight now," he said.

"If the Signore can win over the gate-keeper, he is safe."

"Farewell," I cried, touching Hawk-wood with my heel.

The man's answer was drowned in the noise of the horse's hoofs. I knew from the position of the moon that it must be considerably past the middle of the night. The streets were entirely deserted; not even a watchman seemed to be abroad. Would I still, I wondered, be favored of fortune?

It was not long before I drew up at the door of the gate-house. Without dis-mounting, I smote upon the oak re-peatedly with the hilt of my sword.

"Keeper!" I shouted. "What, ho, there!"

"A thousand curses on you!" cried a voice. "This is the fifth time I have been roused this night. I will see you in the pit before I will open the gates for you."

"Not for five bright gold florins?"

"Five florins!"

"Aye! they are yours if you will

but undo the fastenings and let me ride forth."

" But the laws."

" A rotten fig for the laws ! Who will ever be the wiser ? Are you so rich that you can scorn these yellow comrades ? " and I jingled the gold in my hand.

" I'll come down ! I'll come down at once, Signore."

And so it was that I rode out of Brescia.

Chapter VIII

The Mission to Milan

IT had been my intention in reporting the success of my quest to Gian Galeazzo to explain to him the situation in which Signor Canaro and his daughter were placed, and ask him if he could not in some way intervene in their behalf, but when I entered the presence of my master he gave me no opportunity to broach that which was uppermost in my mind. Del Verme was with him as usual.

"You come in good time, Della Verria," said the Lord of Pavia. "We were wishing you might arrive to-day. What said the captain?"

"That he hoped within a week you would see him in Pavia. He will come as soon as he has accomplished his mission in Brescia, whither I was obliged to go in search of him."

"Excellent! most excellent! I congratulate you. You found him in Brescia, you say? Truly you are as nimble as Mercury."

"Mercury is reputed to have wings, which I have not, but I have a most noble steed, thanks to your Lordship."

"There will be an early occasion for you to use him again, — to-morrow in fact, — when I shall have a little packet for you to deliver to my gracious uncle who rules in Milan. Until then I shall not need you."

This was clearly a dismissal, and I did not think it wise to ask my master to listen to me when he was so evidently desirous of consulting with Del Verme.

"There will come an opportunity soon," I thought; "if not, I will make one," for I was determined that if any word from me could loosen the coils which seemed to be tightening about the lovely Brescia maiden and her father, that word should at all hazards be spoken. I had little more than an inkling of the tragic order in which events were shaping themselves, and did not realize how soon all necessity for appealing to any one in behalf of Signor and Angela Canaro would apparently be obviated.

Repairing to the room in the palace which had been assigned to me, I removed from my person the stain and dust of travel, and then cast myself upon my cot. After two hours I rose much refreshed, and sallied forth in search of Rupert Hartzheim. Finding him off duty, we set out into the town together, and over a hearty supper at a hostelry near the Ticino bridge I related to my friend my experiences during my search for Ardotti. If he was bored by my youthful enthusiasm over my success, he did not show it, and although there was a merry twinkle in his eyes as he listened to my glowing description of Angela Canaro, he forbore to rally me, which, as I now think of it, was most kind of him. He must have seen that my ecstasies were those of a lover (I now admitted to myself that I was in love, though acknowledging the hopelessness of my passion), and surely there is no more tempting mark for pleasantry than the enamoured swain who persists in pouring his raptures into the ears of his friends !

When I told Hartzheim that I had resolved to appeal to Gian Galeazzo in behalf of Signor Canaro and his daughter he made no immediate answer.

" What could he do to aid them ? " he said at length.

" I confess that I cannot see," I replied ; " but possibly he might do something. I shall certainly speak with him when I return from Milan."

" From Milan ! "

" Yes, I am to ride thither on the morrow with some communication from Gian Galeazzo to his uncle."

" Zounds ! " cried Hartzheim, smiting his knee with his palm, " the Visconti of Pavia send a greeting to the tyrant of Milan ! What in the name of wonder may that mean ? "

" You can guess much better than I," I answered.

"It means much, I'll stake a month's pay! Mayhap if you wait a bit there'll be no occasion for your appealing to Gian Galeazzo in behalf of the fair damsel and her father."

"Have you heard anything new at the palace?"

"No, but the Lord of Pavia is not keeping such a force armed and drilled for nothing, and under such a leader as Del Verme. This mission of yours to Milan will bring matters to a head, or I'm a poor prophet!"

It was my opinion that Hartzheim was a good prophet, and filled with a pardonable feeling of pride that I had been chosen as the bearer of what might prove so important a communication, I rode into the palace courtyard the next morning. I had thrown Hawkwood's bridle to a groom, and was about to ascend the main staircase of the palace when I saw Gian Galeazzo and Del Verme coming down the steps together.

"Ah!" said the Lord of Pavia, in his pleasantest manner, as he acknowledged my salute, "our ambassador waits."

"He is quite ready, your Lordship," said I.

"Here is what you are to deliver to my uncle," said he, handing me a small case of soft leather tied with threads of gold. "It contains a topaz of much brilliancy, which I am sending with my respectful homage, and a request in writing to which you are to bring an answer. Shall we tell Della Verria the tenor of the request, Del Verme?"

"It might possibly be a help to him to know," answered the soldier.

"I am sending word to my gracious uncle," said Gian Galeazzo, giving a peculiar emphasis to the last two words which might not have been over-pleasing to the ears of that personage had he heard them, "that three days hence I shall undertake a pilgrimage to the shrine of our Lady of the Mountain, at Varese, and I am beseeching him, inasmuch as my natural timidity disinclines me to enter Milan, to meet me at the parting of the roads without the city in order that I may embrace him and renew those expressions of affection for him which of late years I have had no chance to utter. So ardently have I urged my request that I am hoping you will return with a favorable reply."

I bestowed the packet in my doublet, and turned to mount Hawkwood.

"A word of warning, Della Verria," added the Visconti, "although it may not be necessary. Recall what I said to you before you set out for Mantua, and keep a close tongue."

"Bernabo Visconti shall learn nothing from me that he does not already know," said I.

It was little more than mid-morning when I rode into Milan. I had visited the city several times with my father, and was sufficiently familiar with it to find my way to the palace of Bernabo without stopping to inquire the route thither. Just within the Vercellina gate, however, I came upon an inn in front of which a stream of running water flowed into a great stone basin. As I paused to let

Hawkwood thrust his nose into the cool flood, the landlord came to the door and asked me if I would not enter and refresh myself. It seemed a well-favored hostelry, and as I detected several loiterers within, it occurred to me that I might pick up a few scraps of gossip in regard to the ruling tyrant who, as report had it, was most cordially hated by those whom he governed, so I allowed myself to be persuaded to alight.

"A fine animal you have there," said the landlord, eying Hawkwood with the look of one who was a judge of horse-flesh.

"That he is!" said I. "He has brought me hither from Pavia right quickly."

"Ah, from Pavia!" exclaimed the landlord. "You are a native of that town perhaps?"

"Yes," I returned, "Pavia is my home, though I have lived there but little of late."

I was in no wise forgetting my master's warning, but I knew that I must appear to be voluble and communicative in order to induce the landlord and the others to talk.   It was easy to gabble, and yet in reality to reveal nothing.

"Gentlemen," said I presently to two or three burghers who were within ear-shot, "will you not join me in a flagon of wine?   Mine host keeps an excellent vintage."

Two citizens — tradesmen seemingly — accepted my invitation, and the landlord stood by as we quaffed our liquor.

"To your health," said they.

"To your fair city," said I.

"God send us a better ruler," put in the landlord, *sotto voce*.

"Amen to that!" exclaimed both burghers.

"Rulers are a necessary evil," said I.

"Such a one as ours is a curse!" cried the landlord, and the two citizens nodded assent.   "You have one of the same breed in Pavia, but rumor says there is as much difference between Bernabo and Gian Gale-azzo Visconti as there is between black and white."

"For aught I know that may be," said

I, "yet rumor is ever a jade, and little to be trusted. It has been my experience that go where you will, — Mantua, Bologna, Firenze, — the citizens of each town will tell you they have the worst of rulers. Now, though I make no pretence of having a knowledge of such matters, I'll wager that you have as good a ruler as any of these cities."

"He is a very Satan!" exclaimed the landlord.

"And there is one of his sons, Mastino, whom men call Il Brutto [the ugly], who is the very prince of devils!" cried one of the burghers.

"Young sir," said the other citizen, leaning forward, "there is not in all Italy a match for this pair. Have you never heard of the hounds of Bernabo? He has more than a thousand of them in kennels both within and without the city. To-day is one of the days of reckoning with the keepers — Heaven help the poor men! If a dog dies, the man who has had him in charge is fined his entire property, and flogged well-nigh to death. If a dog is found to be too fat or too lean, the keeper, in either instance, is punished with revolting cruelty. Father and son will be in rare spirits to-day. They have work on hand which is wholly to their liking."

This tale in regard to Bernabo's hounds was not new to my ears, but I had hitherto given little thought to it. That it was true I had not the least doubt. The narrator's earnestness was sufficient confirmation of its dread reality.

"You have heard but one thing," said the man, seeming to take it for granted by my silence that I was sceptical in regard to the truth of his story.

"It is quite sufficient," said I, rising, and walking toward the door, "to make me curious to see this remarkable ruler of yours."

"See him!" cried they, starting to their feet in astonishment.

"Yes," said I; "why not?"

They began looking at one another in a puzzled fashion, wondering whether I were joking or no, and never for a moment dreaming that I was really on my way to seek an audience with Bernabo Visconti. They gathered in the doorway and watched me mount.

"Good day, gentlemen," I cried, waving my hand to them. "I am for the palace." And I left them gaping after me in mute amazement.

I marvelled somewhat that these men had been so outspoken in regard to the ruler of their city to me, a total stranger, but finally came to a conclusion not far short of the truth that the people were fast becoming desperate under the oppression to which they were subjected. An expression of dissatisfaction, of unrest, of dormant rebellion, was plainly to be seen on many faces that were lifted to mine as I rode through the streets. The time was evidently ripe for a change, and I fancied that any one who would, either by force or strategy, overthrow the power of the despotic Bernabo would be hailed with acclaim as a liberator. Was this the part that my master was planning to play? Certainly everything now tended to make me believe such was the case. My heart quickened at the thought. With Gian Galeazzo Lord of Milan new possibilities opened before me, and with the vision of wealth and fame there rose another far fairer—one which I had not been able long to banish since the first time my eyes had rested upon it. That was but a few brief days ago, and yet how great a period it seemed!

I found the piazza, which Gian Galeazzo beautified in after years with that cathedral which is the wonder of Europe, flooded with the dazzling spring sunlight. It was well-nigh deserted, and I could but contrast the busy scene which the square in front of my master's palace presented with the ominous quietude which brooded here. Despite the glow of the sunshine it was as though a spirit of blight rested upon the spot.

Two sullen guards stood upon either side of the palace gateway, and as I made bold to ride between them into the court-yard, one of them put his hand upon Hawkwood's bridle and demanded my business. I replied that I desired an audience with his master, but he would not allow me to pass until he had called one from within who questioned me sharply. This man was of middle age, swarthy and keen-eyed, and garbed in a rich dark livery. He finally bade me enter, saying, as he walked at my side, —

"His Lordship has just returned from the kennels, and it may be you will not be able to see him at once. However, I will ascertain."

A serving-man took charge of my horse, and I followed my conductor into the palace. I must confess that my pulses did not flow with their wonted serenity, although outwardly I was calm enough. I realized that I might be about to enter the presence of one of the most unscrupulous and cruel men in all Italy, and although my mission was seemingly innocent, I felt sure that it might possibly be fraught with weighty consequences.

I was left in a small, bare ante-chamber while he who had accompanied me passed into the adjoining apartment. Scarcely had I taken three turns in the narrow room when my guide reappeared.

"His Lordship will see you now," he said.

I stepped through the doorway, and found myself in a large, light reception-hall at the farther end of which, near a tall window, two men were standing. Between them was a huge boar-hound with whose ears the smaller man was toying. Although my spurred heels rang upon the oaken flooring, the two paid no heed to me as I advanced. It was not until my conductor spoke that either so much as noticed my presence, although the dog cast upon me a suspicious glance from his savage eyes.

"This is the gentleman who wishes to see your Lordship."

At these words from my guide the two turned. The younger and smaller of them was tricked out with all the finery of a gallant, and showed as ugly and malicious a face as it had ever been my lot to see. A sneer hovered perpetually about his mouth, and in his eyes there burned a vicious and evil light. It needed no second glance to tell me that this was Mastino Visconti, called Il Brutto by the burgher whom I had encountered at the inn. There was a resemblance between father and son, but the countenance of Bernabo was cast in a larger mould. In it there was less cunning, but more force and daring, yet the sinister stamp was as clear upon it as upon that of the younger man.

Having made my obeisance, I took from my doublet the packet entrusted to me by Gian Galeazzo.

"This," I said, placing it in Bernabo's hand, "my master, your nephew and dutiful son-in-law, bids me give you in token of his earnest regard."

There came from Il Brutto a little ironical laugh that was hollow of mirth, whereat his father cast a questioning eye upon him. Then with a grunt, expressive of what emotion I could not conjecture, he broke the threads which bound the packet, and plucked forth the gem, which he held up to the light.

"A fine stone, by the saints!" said he, and I noticed that his face grew wolfishly avaricious as he gazed at it. Presently he pulled out the writing, which he deliberately unfolded and as slowly scanned. When he looked up, it was to regard me critically from head to toe.

"Why do you serve such a craven as this nephew and son-in-law of mine?" he cried, with a snarl. "You seem a likely looking youth — too likely to be the message-bearer of a coward!"

I bowed my acknowledgments.

"One must serve some one or starve," said I.

"Do you know what this missive contains?" he demanded.

"My master honored me by telling me."

"What do you think," cried he, "of a man who dares not visit his own father's brother, his own wife's father? Dares not! Does he think the city of Milan a den of cutthroats? Body of Christ, that my daughter should have married such a poltroon!" His grizzled upper lip lifted in a sardonic laugh, and his white teeth showed like the boar-hound's fangs.

"May not timidity be a physical infirmity," said I, "for which one should not be held accountable?"

"It can be overcome," thundered Bernabo. "I'll see my cowardly, praying, priest-like nephew and tell him so to his face. By God, I will! 'His natural timidity disinclines him to enter Milan,' does it? Well, he shall have his wish. I will meet him as he desires. Will he have his horde of whining priests with him? I suppose so. A fine company to keep, forsooth!"

Il Brutto touched his father's arm.

"Let me see what my cousin writes," he said.

Bernabo handed him the missive. When he had finished reading it, he scowled and whispered something in his father's ear.

"You are grown amazingly cautious of a sudden," said the Lord of Milan, mockingly. "Here, Marzo," he cried, seizing the letter and holding it toward the man

who had guided me to the apartment;
"you know humanity as well as you know
dogs.   Tell me what you think of this."

The master of Bernabo's hounds — for
he it was—ran his sharp eyes rapidly over
the writing, but his expression did not
change.

" Will your Lordship step aside a moment?" he said, as he looked up.

The three men withdrew several paces
and began conversing in low tones.   I
pretended in the meanwhile to be intent
upon something that was taking place in
the courtyard below, but in reality I was
listening intently to catch some word that
would give me a clew to what was passing
between them.   I felt that both Il Brutto
and Marzo suspected that there was a
hidden motive in Gian Galeazzo's request,
and were urging Bernabo not to meet his
nephew as proposed.   They had, however, an obstinate subject to deal with.

"I tell you he's too much of a coward!"
I heard the Lord of Milan blurt out, with
an impatient snort.

There was more talk in an undertone,

then a string of imprecations burst from Bernabo.

"Am I so old that I am a fool?" he cried, and I realized that they were returning, and wheeled to face them. The Lord of Milan came forward, his cruel face twitching with anger.

"This is my message to your master, my nephew and son-in-law, Gian Galeazzo Visconti," he said, his gruff voice the hoarser from ire. "Tell him that I will meet him at mid-morning, three days hence, without the Vercillina gate where the road branches toward Varese, unless in the meanwhile he has a fit of fear and remains shut up with his priests and clerks."

The evident opposition of Il Brutto and Marzo had availed nothing save to enrage the Milanese despot. The former shrugged his shoulders as though to indicate that he had no further interest in the matter, while the latter kept his penetrating gaze fixed upon my face.

I bowed in response to Bernabo's announcement, making a fitting reply, and then Il Brutto said that he would see me back to the courtyard. He led the way in taciturn silence, and as both his face and manner filled me with loathing I made no attempt at conversation. At the head of the stairway he paused and saluted me stiffly. I saw that it was not his intention to descend, so returned his salute with equal formality and passed downward. As I reached the landing by which the descent was broken, a voice arrested my steps. Looking back, I beheld Marzo above me. Il Brutto had disappeared. As the master of hounds joined me, I noticed that he held in his hand a finely chased chain of gold whereto a pendant was attached in which a large emerald burned like a cat's eye in the dark. He did not fail to let me have a good look at the trinket, and it flashed into my mind that there was method in his so doing.

"You return to Pavia directly?" he said.

"At once."

"Do you find service there agreeable?"

" Most agreeable."

" Ah ! one of your bearing and spirit under a man of no spirit ! It is difficult to understand."

To this I made no reply. We had halted and stood facing one another on the landing, he with his legs wide apart, swinging the gold chain and the gleaming emerald before my eyes. I knew well enough what he was about to propose, and waited with some curiosity to see how he would put it. He did not hesitate long. I certainly had not given him an iota of encouragement, but he went, I presume, on the supposition that every man has his price.

" My Lord, Bernabo Visconti," he began, " has long wished that he could find some one both intelligent and trustworthy who would act as his confidential agent in Pavia. To such an one he would be most generous ; to such an one he would be pleased to present this rare bit of jewelry as a token of his good faith, and as earnest of the reward to follow service faithfully rendered. The man whom he seeks must of necessity have some occupation that would keep him in touch with public affairs, and be in a position that would place him above suspicion. Indeed, if by any chance, he should be in some capacity connected with the ruler of Pavia, it would be exceedingly advantageous. Do you not know of such a person?"

He leaned forward insinuatingly, still dangling the chain and the jewel before me.

"I do not," I said shortly, although I was more amused than angered at so barefaced a proposal.

"Think for a moment!" he went on, seemingly not put out by my decided reply. "To a young man who has his way to make, such an opportunity might mean a fortune. It might prove the chance of a lifetime. Are you still quite sure you know of no one?"

"Yes, quite sure," said I, looking him squarely in the eyes.

"I confess that I am disappointed," said he, still suave, although he now ceased to swing the chain. " I thought you were a youth of discernment, but we all make our mistakes. You had better go back to your sallow-faced coward !"

"You had best keep to your dogs," said I.

His dagger was out in a flash, but I was too quick for him. Down the staircase I flew, three and four steps at a time. Into the courtyard I sprang, and ran toward where Hawkwood was standing. Every second I expected to hear Marzo's voice bidding some of the guardsmen arrest my flight, but no word came. Not until I was upon Hawkwood's back did I look toward the palace doorway. There I saw no sign of the master of Bernabo's hounds, nor did I catch a glimpse of him as I rode out into the piazza.

Chapter IX

The Coup-de-Main

THERE was a great stir in and about the Palazzo Visconti in Pavia on a certain Sabbath afternoon of early May, in the year 1385. News had gone abroad through the city that Gian Galeazzo would, that day, start upon a pilgrimage to the shrine of our Lady at Varese, and a great concourse had assembled to see him depart. In the square upon which the palace looked, five hundred lancers were drawn up to await the Lord of Pavia, half the number upon one side and half upon the other side of the palace entrance. A brave sight they presented as Gian Galeazzo, Del Verme, the captain of the palace guard, and I rode out into the piazza. Line by line, troop by troop, they wheeled into marching order, and in their midst we four passed the gateway of Santa Maria in Portica, and set our faces toward Milan.

I could but think, as we held our way between the fields and orchards, of the change that had come over my life since that day, by no means far distant, when I plodded on foot along the same roadway, trying to think out what line of action I should follow, perplexed and uncertain as regards my future. True, I had made no real progress in that which I had resolved to accomplish, a retraction from my father of the foul slander he had put upon my mother's name, yet I had a feeling that the position I now held would one day help me in carrying out my purpose. Of Angela Canaro and her father, I had as yet said nothing to my master. As I rode back from my mission to Milan, I determined to await the outcome of the Varese pilgrimage before I attempted to solicit Gian Galeazzo's assistance in their behalf. Hartzheim's words, together with the subsequent trend of events, brought me to this decision. There was nothing to be gained — so I told myself — by speaking at once, and a delay, even provided nothing came of the meeting between nephew and uncle, could do no harm to the cause of those in whom I was interested.

There was little talk between Del Verme and the Lord of Pavia as we rode onward, and the captain of the palace guard and I exchanged scarcely a word. Among the men there was no merriment despite the fairness of the sky and of the fields, and although the pennons fluttered somewhat gayly overhead, and there was a silvery jingling of spurs and a martial clatter of harness, our cavalcade had in every respect the air of a company setting out to do homage at a distant shrine. Yet I am very sure religious thoughts stirred not a single heart in all that grave array.

Our pace was never beyond a gentle amble, as befitted the day and my master's announced intent, and it was well toward evening before we reached the outskirts of Benasco, at which place we planned to pass the night. The mayor of the municipality with his associates came forth to greet us, and conducted Gian Galeazzo to the house of the chief magistrate, where he was to be entertained. The men bivouacked in the public buildings and the castle, which was the property of the Visconti, and the officers were quartered with some of the leading citizens. That evening, with a specially selected escort, my master attended vespers at the chief church of Benasco, gave a large offering of alms, and appeared to be particularly earnest in his devotions. It was then, so I afterwards heard, that he made a vow to the Virgin, binding himself, should the expedition prove favorable, to erect some holy edifice. Out of this vow grew the stately Certosa di Pavia.

When we rode from the town the next morning, my place was with Del Verme and my master well in the van of the troops. In fact, but forty lancers, commanded by Hartzheim, preceded us, ten lines with four men abreast. Thus were we disposed when Hartzheim, who had been riding in advance, galloped back to announce that two richly arrayed horsemen were approaching.

"Very likely they are the bearers of messages from your uncle to your Lordship," said the German.

"Conduct them to me when they come up," said my master, and Hartzheim hastened away to execute his order.

"When they approach, seize and disarm them whoever they are!" exclaimed my master, addressing Del Verme.

"It shall be as you command," answered the soldier, who bade me give the lancers about us the necessary directions.

The lines in front of us now opened, and between them came Hartzheim, conducting two middle-aged men of evident rank.

"Ah, cousins, a fair greeting!" cried Gian Galeazzo when he saw them.

"A fair greeting to you!" cried they, in return; but before they could speak further they were suddenly set upon by the lancers nearest them and disarmed before they could offer the least resistance. In vain they protested to Gian Galeazzo, who, without the least exhibition of feeling, ordered them to be taken to the rear.

Thus did Ludovico and Rodolfo Visconti disappear from the public stage.

For some time we had been able to see the spires of Milan, and now as the walls came plainly into view my master began to show signs of nervousness. He moved uneasily in his saddle, and as I cast a look at him covertly from the corner of my eye I noticed that his face had assumed the colorless, pasty appearance it had worn during the early part of my memorable first meeting with him. Hartzheim had sent back word that a number of mounted men were approaching, and Del Verme had ridden forward to view them. He returned shortly with the announcement, —

"It is your Lordship's uncle. His escort numbers only about twenty-five. The affair will be an easy matter."

The Visconti's countenance gained a little color at this, yet he was still visibly anxious.

"Keep near me, Della Verria," he said, "and have your eyes open."

There was not a shadow of doubt in regard to what was about to happen.

Bernabo Visconti was to be made a prisoner.

We had now approached a building of considerable size, the hospital of San Ambrosio, which stood near where the roadway branched toward Varese. The lancers in front of us halted, and then the whole troop came to a standstill. As those in the van wheeled their horses to one side, we descried the figure of Bernabo Visconti, mounted upon a white mule, riding several paces in advance of his attendants. Onward he came between the array of spears, seemingly unsuspicious of his fate. I looked keenly among those who followed him, but discovered neither the evil face of Il Brutto nor the dark countenance of the master of hounds.

Gian Galeazzo, Del Verme, and several others, myself among the number, had dismounted to receive the Lord of Milan. As two guardsmen grasped the bridle of his mule and Bernabo sprang to the ground, my master with outstretched arms and pleasant words advanced toward his uncle, who suffered himself to be embraced.

But before on his part a syllable had been spoken, and while uncle and nephew had scarcely yet parted from their embrace, I heard my master's voice ring out as I had never heard it before — "*Strike!*"

At that instant a clarion sounded, and while the lancers swiftly encompassed the astonished and discomfited Milanese, Del Verme presented his sword at Bernabo's breast and informed him that he was a prisoner.

The whole thing was so quickly, so quietly, so masterfully done, that not a drop of blood was shed, and not one of the tyrant's escort escaped. In less than half an hour we were at the Vercellina gate, and not a hand was lifted to oppose our triumphal entry. From street to street, from house to house, as by aerial magic, spread the news, and by the time we reached the piazza and the ancient palace of the Della Torre a throng had gathered that, with unmistakable acclamations of joy, hailed Gian Galeazzo as their deliverer.

Signs and omens were not lacking in the

heavens at this time, foretelling that some great event was about to take place; for, according to Pietro Azario, a learned notary of Novara, Saturn, Jupiter, and Mars were then in the House of the Twins; and, eight days previous, a furious bolt of lightning cast down from the summit of Bernabo's palace that stood over against the church of San Georgio, a gilded viper, the ensign of the house of the Visconti.

Chapter X

The Last March of Bernabo

NOT many days after the seizure of Bernabo Visconti, and the triumphal entry of Gian Galeazzo into Milan, a troop of fifty men-at-arms gathered in the courtyard of the palace which had formerly been the chief residence of the Milan despot. My master had already transferred his household from Pavia, those of Bernabo's retainers who had not fled had either been sent into exile or imprisoned, and Gian Galeazzo had been proclaimed the ruler of the city. Many of the towns that had formerly owed allegiance to Bernabo had hastened to swear fealty to the new lord, and each succeeding day gave evidence that throughout Lombardy, wherever the news spread, folk hailed with delight the change so subtly and bloodlessly wrought.

In the centre of the troop of men-at-arms, all of whom were mounted, his arms pinioned to his sides, sat a man who for many a year had inspired fear not only within the walls of the fair city which he ruled, but throughout all the fertile region over which his dominion extended. To what was passing about him he gave no heed. With head half bent, and eyes fixed and vacant, he seemed unconscious of the curious scrutiny of the troopers who surrounded him. Only once did I notice any shade of emotion upon his face, and this was when he raised his eyes and found me sitting upon Hawkwood at his left. Then, with the look of recognition, there came a sharp contraction of his heavy brows, which instantly disappeared as he glanced at Hartzheim stationed upon his other side. Presently Del Verme emerged from the palace, mounted, and placed himself at the head of the troop. As we rode from the courtyard into the piazza a low murmur rose from the crowd there awaiting our appearance, a murmur that swelled into a shout of exultation. If Bernabo was stirred by the outcry, no line of his countenance showed it. He did not even glance toward the sea of faces that heaved about us in such a passionate mingling of hate and joy, — hate of the fallen tyrant, and joy that his power was at an end. The young and the old, the high and the low, one and all, regardless of condition or sex, from street, from window, and from housetop, flung their taunts and their execrations at the deposed tyrant. But not until we had passed beyond the walls did the feeling which the acts of Bernabo had inspired become fully evident. As we turned our faces toward Monza we saw, dotted here and there for some distance, groups of peasants who had gathered by the roadside. As we neared the first group, which was composed of both men and women, perhaps a dozen in number, a shrill outcry was raised, the voices of the women mounting high above those of the men, fierce, clamorous, and vindictive.

"Let us see the face of the devil! Let us see how he looks!" they cried, pressing close to us, and searching eagerly for him who rode in our midst. When they saw Bernabo, with his arms pinioned and his head averted, mighty was the shout that went up. Another group now came hastening toward us, unable, in their eagerness to gaze upon their persecutor in his abasement, to wait until we had reached them. A woman led them, wild of eye and with streaming hair. With gleeful cries and frantic motions of her arms she bade her companions hurry on.

"There he is!" she shrieked, flinging a long skinny finger at Bernabo. "I should know him in the blackest night. O you fiend out of hell, you shall behold your work!"   Into the crowd she plunged and drew one forth by the hand whose face was a horror to see, for where the eyes had been stared two burned and blackened holes.

"Look! look!" the woman cried, in a voice so commanding that even Bernabo was constrained to gaze toward her; "this is my son, my only son.   What crime did he commit?   What wrong did he do? none! but two dogs of which he had charge sickened and died, and you must have his eyes plucked out.   Curse him, my son!"

"Aye! curse him with me!" exclaimed a stalwart fellow, lifting the stump of his right arm as he hurled an awful imprecation at Bernabo.

"And with me!" another cried, who, to keep pace with us, made desperate leaps upon his crutch over the uneven ground.

So for a mile and more this pitiful scene was enacted.   At first it seemed to have but little effect upon our prisoner, but after a time I perceived that he began to shake like one having the ague or palsy.   He gnawed his lip, he glanced apprehensively from side to side as though he feared that the enraged men and women would burst through our ranks, drag him from his horse, and rend him in pieces. Indeed, I could but feel that this was the fate he deserved.

It was a vast relief when we at length

left the last group of the wronged and maimed behind. The sights I had witnessed, the tales I had heard, were burned deep into my brain, and I began to wonder if the man by whose side I rode was not some incarnation of evil sent upon earth to scourge humanity. As for Hartzheim, I noticed that he shrank away from Bernabo as though he were one afflicted with the black death.

It lacked yet an hour of noon when we rode into Monza. Our appearance, however, created but little stir in the streets, for Bernabo was not recognized. True, one of the troopers bore the ensign of Gian Galeazzo, the ensign which later was to inspire dread throughout entire northern Italy, but it then stood for nothing in the eyes of the beholders. The design was that of a serpent from whose mouth was issuing a naked child. This it was that, in after time, caused Gian Galeazzo Visconti to be called the Great Serpent, or the Great Viper, *Il Biscione*.

We had just debouched into the piazza, and were riding in loose rank, save the few of us who were directly about Bernabo, when a dull sound as of the hoofs of many horses came suddenly to my ear.

"What is that?" I called to Hartzheim, as I reined Hawkwood.

He, too, had heard the noise, as had others among our comrades, and there were curious glances cast in the direction from which it proceeded. None of us, however, dreamed what was about to occur. Del Verme's attention was now attracted by the growing sound, and he had little more than given the order to close ranks when a band of thirty horsemen burst into the square a little in advance upon our right, and charged at full tilt diagonally down upon us.

We had come forth anticipating no such encounter, and there were not more than a dozen lances among us, while there were twice that number in the attacking party, so while we had fifty men and they but thirty, they had at the outset the distinct advantage. Moreover, many of us had donned only the very lightest body armor, while our assailants were armed cap-a-pie.

Scarcely had our dozen lancers time to form in front for the protection of the rest of our troop when our foe was upon us, and we were borne backward by the impetus of the onset.

"A rescue! a rescue!" was the cry they raised, and I heard Del Verme shout above the din of the mêlée, —

"Look out for the prisoner!"

Indeed, I had quite forgotten him in the suddenness of the attack, and now that I turned to look at him I found his mien had changed from that of sullen submission to that of enraged resistance. He was tugging fiercely at the bonds that pinioned his arms, and was galling the horse he bestrode so viciously with the stirrup that the animal plunged and snorted and threatened to do serious injury.

"Be quiet, you hound of hell!" I heard Hartzheim cry, as he flashed his sword before Bernabo's eyes. Then I realized that I must have a care for my own safety.

At the first onrush I had been so hedged about by others that none of the foe came near me, but now that our ranks had in a measure been broken, the men were fighting in little groups, and against those of us about Bernabo the most desperate attack was presently directed. Lances had been cast aside, and we were engaged with our swords hand to hand. So many of our troop had been unhorsed or slain in the first contact that we now fought with almost equal numbers; indeed it seemed to me that the fortune of the day appeared to be going against us. I could hear Del Verme's shouts of cheer from the other side of the press, and see-ing Hartzheim had pushed his way to a place upon my left, I concluded that he had given Bernabo into another's charge. Presently there was such a bickering of steel as I had never before known, the like of which I was not to behold again in many a day. Had not Hartzheim been close at hand to encourage and aid me I doubt if I should have come off as well as I did; for despite all my training and instruction at his hands, I was far from being wholly at home in the saddle. I owed much also to Hawkwood, who seemed, undirected, always to make the right move.

My comrade and I had just given two lusty fellows so sharp a taste of our blades that they were glad to rein to the edge of the fray, when I saw two riders forcing their way toward us, cutting right and left as they came. The beavers of both men were raised, and I recognized them instantly. They were the leaders of the attack, Il Brutto, Bernabo's son, and Marzo, his master of the hounds. I had not more than time to communicate to Hartzheim who they were ere they were upon us. Marzo was my antagonist, and he assailed me with a ferocity I had never before encountered. Almost unprotected as I was by armor, a light coat of linked mail being the only bit of harness that I wore, it seemed for a few seconds that I was doomed, but the fact that I was unincumbered really proved my salvation. Though the force of my antagonist's strokes several times came near beating down my guard, the complete freedom of my arm enabled me the more readily to parry, while I could twist and turn and bend unhampered by the cumbersome plates and joints of steel. Had I been on foot, and had the man opposed to me been as I was, but lightly protected, despite his terrible strength I should not have felt compelled to stand so entirely upon the defensive. I should not have wondered, as I now did, how long it would be before he would overpower me by sheer might. My suppleness, my nimbleness, would have told for something more than mere evasion.

I could see that my resistance was fast working Marzo into a more fiery rage. He flung out an awful oath.

"By the blood of Christ!" said he; "what power protects you?"

I saw him rise in his stirrups, and my blade went up to meet the downward rush of his steel. But the blow never came. I was conscious of a gleaming line of light and an arm thrust between us. As Hawkwood swerved to make room for the horse of Hartzheim, out from under Marzo's gorget came a bright spurt of blood, and

The Death of the Master of the Hounds. — Page 146

the body of Bernabo's master of hounds fell forward upon the neck of his steed, a limp and lifeless thing.

Il Brutto had already fled discomfited, and with his disappearance and Marzo's death the soul animating the attack was gone. The others soon took to their heels.

A sorry sight was the piazza of Monza after the flight of our assailants. Presently the terrified townsfolk ventured out and assisted us in removing the bodies of the dead and in caring for the wounded. Leaving those who were unable to mount in the charge of some of the kindly-hearted citizens, our thinned and scarred troop rode forward with our prisoner in our midst. Bernabo's mood had again become that of sullen dejection, and scarcely once through the long hours of our march did he raise his head, not even when we passed through the gateway of the fortress of Trezzo, which he himself had caused to be raised on the banks of the rushing Adda, from which he never reappeared to the eyes of man.

Chapter XI

The Face at the Casement

SOON after Gian Galeazzo Visconti was established as Lord of Milan, he entered into a league with the Lord of Padua, the Marquis of Ferrara, and the Marquis of Mantua, for the purpose of freeing Italy from the companies of German, French, and English mercenaries, that, under the nominal employ of various petty princes, had incited wars and devastated country and town in wanton pillage. Great things were hoped for as the outcome of this confederation. A banner with a blue field was chosen, whereupon the inscription "Pax" was emblazoned. A new era was to be inaugurated, an era of peace and good will. In this movement my master was the impelling force, and at first no one questioned his sincerity. His well-known timidity, his apparent love of justice, his fondness for quiet and scholarly pursuits, made it seem natural that he should wish to live in amity with all men. His overthrow of Bernabo was looked upon merely as a matter of self-preservation.

Upon the business of the league I was despatched far and near, and one of my first missions was to Padua, whither I was sent with important letters to the lord of the city, Francesco da Carrara. When Gian Galeazzo gave me his commands, my heart leaped with delight, and for two reasons. Padua had been my mother's home, and I deemed that there, if anywhere, I should be able to get some trace of the surviving members of her family. To them I intended to make myself known, and through them I hoped to come to an understanding of my father's unnatural and, I felt sure, unfounded aspersions upon my mother's memory.

The other reason for the quickening of my pulse was the fact that my journey would take me through Brescia, whither my thoughts had daily turned during the weeks that had elapsed since my adventurous experiences there. Perhaps I should see Angela Canaro again! Certainly I should make bold to call upon her father, to express my regret at Ardotti's sad end, the news of which came soon after my master's entry into Milan, and hope whispered in my ear that possibly there might be a second face to give me greeting at the palace of the Canari.

But my fair anticipations were destined to be frosted by disappointment. Signor Canaro was not in Brescia, and when I ventured to ask the servant who answered my summons if his master were likely to be long absent (I had it in my mind that perhaps I might find him when I rode back from Padua), the evasive reply I received showed me that my inquiries were regarded with suspicion. Recalling that on my first visit to Brescia, Signorina Canaro had just returned from Verona, I haunted the streets and public places of the latter city a whole day in the hope of getting a glimpse of father or daughter. It was in vain that I did so. And yet, notwithstanding my lack of success, it was only the urgency of my mission that prevented me from continuing the search.

At Padua another blow awaited me. I learned that my mother's only surviving near relative was a cousin, the son of the uncle and aunt by whom she had been reared, one who had been a wanderer for years, returning to his home only at rare intervals. From the steward who had charge of his property — for he still had interests in Padua — I ascertained that he was at present somewhere in Germany, the man could not say exactly where, as he had received no communication from him for several months. The best that I could do was to despatch a letter to my cousin, acquainting him with my existence (of which I was by no means sure he was aware, since during my recollection there had been no communication between my father and my mother's kin) and with my earnest desire to see him, and begging him when he should return to Padua, to inform me of the fact. This done, and my mission to Francesco da Carrara accomplished, I set my face disconsolately toward Milan.

Had I had time, at this juncture, to indulge in much reflection, I doubt not I should have given myself over to melancholy; but hardly had I returned and made my report to Gian Galeazzo before I was again bidden to ride forth. So for several months after my mission to Padua I had little chance to brood over my ill-success in seeing the lady of my heart and in finding the last representative of my mother's family. But at length there came a period of inaction. I was no longer sent hither and yon upon the business of the league. The confederation which had promised so fairly at the outset, upon which all those really interested in the prosperity and peace of Italy based such high hopes, seemed likely to fail, to be completely abandoned. The cause of its failure, so I one day heard my master aver, was the jealousy and suspicion with which its promoters regarded one another.

Gian Galeazzo professed himself to be entirely free from any such feeling, and placed the blame entirely upon his confederates; but I, who had seen much of the inner workings of the league, was not to be deceived by his words. In fact, I soon made up my mind that it was the Visconti alone who was responsible for the dissolution of the confederation.

This discovery did not add to my happiness. Up to this time I had looked upon my master as a man of honor, one whose ambitions were higher than the other rulers of the day, who had in view the good of those whom he governed. I had always realized that his nature was shrewd and calculating rather than sympathetic, but his intentions I had never mistrusted. Now I began to see that he was avaricious both of wealth and power. Before many months I was to learn that he was totally unscrupulous. The pleasure and pride I had always taken in serving him were gone, and I grew moody and discontented.

Hartzheim rallied me for what he called my visionary ideas.

"They are all the same, these lords and princes," said he. "I could have told you what you now know long ago."

But in spite of my friend's bantering, and the general good cheer which he suffused, my spirits continued under a cloud. The future looked dark. I heard nothing from Padua; I had almost ceased to hope that I should ever see Angela Canaro again, although I thought of her by day and dreamed of her by night; and as for my father, from him came neither word nor sign to show that he cared whether I were living or dead.

One afternoon late in the winter of 1387, when the heat of the sun had begun to temper the dampness and chill of the air, as I was leaving the palace in search of Hartzheim, it chancing that we were both off duty, I encountered three horsemen with their attendants about halting at the gateway. In the foremost of the riders I recognized a man whom I had seen at the court of the Lord of Padua, one high in the councils of that ruler. Later in the day I met him again — this time passing through one of the corridors of the palace in earnest conversation with my master.

"Are they going to attempt to revive the league," I thought, "or is something else on foot?"

The strangers remained two days in Milan, then rode away, and they passed from my mind until a morning two weeks later when I was summoned into Gian Galeazzo's presence.

"You have been low-spirited of late, Della Verria," he said; "though I have seen little of you that has not escaped me. Inaction, I know, is like a disease to young blood, and I have called you to me to set you riding again, even as far as Padua."

My master smiled as he noted the look of pleasure that crossed my face.

"It is good news to you, I see," he remarked.

"It is indeed," I said, leaving him to infer that the cause of my manifest delight was the thought of being once more in the saddle.

"I should like to have you start at once. Here is a letter which you are to deliver to Francesco da Carrara, or to his son, Francesco Novello. You shall not lack for that which will stir your blood now, Della Verria. I remember once hearing you say that you did not wish to remain behind if there were active service in the field. Well, you shall soon have your desire."

I did not need to have the meaning of these words explained to me. The men from Padua had been ambassadors from Francesco da Carrara, to solicit the assistance of Gian Galeazzo against Antonio della Scala of Verona, with whom the Lord of Padua had been engaged in conflict for nearly a year. I was to be the bearer of the missive announcing the Visconti's decision to render the requested aid. Had I but known what was erelong to happen, with how earnest a warning against such an alliance would I have delivered this letter; for Francesco da

Carrara was a noble prince, one who in no wise deserved to be drawn into the snares that Gian Galeazzo finally wove for his undoing! But I was no seer, and could not read the stars, nor could I detect the subtle schemes that had begun to take form within my master's brain.

"Your Lordship has ever been most gracious to me," I said.

"There may be greater rewards than you have dreamed of in store for you, if you continue to serve me well."

I thanked my master, deep in my heart the while regretting that I had lost faith in his truth and high purpose.

"Here is another missive which I shall ask you to deliver on your way to Padua," said the Visconti, holding out to me a second folded and sealed slip of parchment. "It is to be given to a citizen of Brescia, a man well known, so that you will have no difficulty in finding his residence. His name, as you will see by the superscription, is Vincenzo Canaro."

It was well that I glanced down at the letter, as Gian Galeazzo referred to the address, else had he surely seen by the expression of my countenance that the name was not new to my ears. Why, I cannot say, there now came over me a feeling of relief at the thought that I had never appealed to my master in behalf of Signor Canaro and his daughter, — that Gian Galeazzo was not aware that I had any knowledge of their existence.

My mind was busy with conjectures in regard to what the second missive might contain as I bowed myself from my master's presence, and went to prepare for my journey. Yet, puzzle as I would over the matter, I could arrive at no satisfactory conclusion. One thing, however, seemed likely; namely, that Signor Canaro was in Brescia, and that I would see him. Should I see the lovely face of his daughter as well, and, if so, would she remember me? Again, as many times before, my breast was torn by fears, — fears that her heart, and indeed her hand, might by this time have been given to another. "Oh, you fond fool," I had often said to myself, "how can you be so senseless as to imagine that in the brief meeting at her home she bestowed upon you more than the polite attention she would naturally give to a guest!" And yet each time I thus upbraided my folly there came back to my memory her look at parting. Truly the doting lover will pin his hopes upon the most intangible things!

Hawkwood was as glad as I to be out under the blue vault of the sky once more, and famous was the progress that we made. As we passed, at the verge of noon, through the outskirts of Treviglio, I noticed in the stable yard of a well-kept little inn two sleek-limbed horses and two fine palfreys. "Some people of quality are riding abroad," I thought; and, glancing at the inn windows, I had a flitting view of a face at one of the upper casements. The sight startled me, and I reined Hawkwood, but I saw no further sign of the occupant of the room though I scrutinized the casement several minutes. I was half minded to pause at the inn for refreshments instead of at one further on, where I had formerly been well served;

but finally, with a smile at what seemed my foolish fancy, I rode on. The face at the window had reminded me of Angela Canaro. Had I yielded to my impulse, how different might have been the after pages of this history !

That evening, for the third time, I stood looking at the arms of the Canari above the palace entrance while I waited for an answer to my summons.

"Is Signor Canaro within?" I asked of the servant who presently appeared. "I have a missive for him from the Lord of Milan."

"Signor Canaro left for Milan on the afternoon of yesterday," was the reply I received. "He was to pass the night at Chiari, and should by this time have reached his destination."

"And the Signorina?" I exclaimed, amazed and disappointed at the news.

"Accompanied him, Signore."

Then it had not been my imagination. It *was* the face of Angela Canaro that I had seen at the casement of the inn at Treviglio !

Chapter XII

At Padua

ON the evening of the following
day but one I wandered out into
the streets of Padua. I had delivered the
communication from my master into the
hands of Francesco da Carrara, and had
endeavored vainly to find my cousin's
steward. He had left the city for a day
or two. Should I await his return, and
endeavor to learn if he knew anything
more definite in regard to my cousin's
whereabouts? Reason said that this was
the thing to do, yet something in my
heart urged me back to Milan. I had
been unable to dismiss the Treviglio incident from my mind, and a hundred times
had I upbraided my perverseness in not
following my impulse to stop at the inn.

My only solace was the thought that Angela Canaro and her father were at Milan. I told myself that I was pretty sure to get trace of them, inasmuch as all indication pointed to some matter of common interest (and of considerable importance) between my master and Signor Canaro — what, I was wholly at a loss to imagine. Sooner or later I was likely to encounter the Brescian noble at the palace, if I did not chance upon him elsewhere.

While I was thus ruminating I gave small heed to whither my steps were leading me, and did not realize that I had strayed into a little-frequented street. There was a half moon in a clear sky, and the air was soft with the first breath of spring. As I passed the entrance to an alley-way that was packed with gloom, I grew suddenly conscious of a sense of danger. But the intuition came too late to enable me to escape unharmed. I have always believed, however, that it saved my life, for the movement which I involuntarily made caused the blow, which otherwise must have crushed my head to a jelly, to fall obliquely. I reeled against the wall, vainly clutching at it with one hand for support, while with the other I recall that I attempted to draw my sword. Then there came a black blur before my eyes, and I thought myself falling, falling, through bottomless depths of space.

A bright light that dazed me when I tried to look at it brought me to a realization of regained consciousness. I felt myself lifted and borne along some distance. Then there came a halt, and I heard the swinging back of doors. Soon I knew that I was being carried up a stairway, then the arms that had held me so firmly were loosened, and I was laid upon a couch which seemed so deliciously soft that I remember thinking it must be eider-down.

Another day had come when I once more opened my eyes. The room in which I found myself was lofty and spacious. There were rich tapestries upon the walls, and the ceiling was beautifully decorated with a fresco of vines and flowers. The couch which had seemed so soft the night before proved to be a great bedstead elaborately carved. I raised myself upon my elbow and looked about me. There was no one in the room. I saw my clothes upon a chair near the bed, and after sitting up, and finding that I had lost but little strength, I began slowly to get into them. I was dizzy at first, but, as I progressed, this feeling passed away. I took a swallow of wine from a decanter which stood upon the table, and presently, when I had bathed my head, which, in one particular spot, was painfully sore, I felt quite myself, save for a slight unsteadiness when I tried to walk.

While I was contemplating which of the two doors issuing from the apartment I should try, one of them softly opened, and a man stood upon the threshold. He was of middle age, and though tall and erect had the air of the scholar rather than that of the soldier. There was a singular winningness in his whole face, despite the deep lines of sadness and restlessness about his eyes. I felt drawn toward him in a way which I could not understand.

That my host and rescuer — for such I

at once conceived him to be — was surprised to find me dressed and upon my feet, his face clearly showed.

"A wise young man," said he, with a grave smile, "after receiving such a blow as you got last night, would have kept his bed at least till noon."

"I never made any pretence to wisdom," I replied; "but of gratitude, Signore, my heart is full."

He waved his hand to silence my expression of thanks.

"It was unfortunate," he said, "that I did not arrive sooner upon the scene. I fancy the rascals who attacked you had already relieved you of whatever valuables you had about your person, and had left you for dead."

"They are quite welcome to my purse," I answered, "for I have more gold in my doublet, and to all my rings, save one which was my mother's."

"Your mother is not living, then?" my rescuer said softly. "You will pardon the question, I hope, if I ask you who your mother was, and if you are said to resemble her? Your face —" he hesitated as though moved by some strong emotion — "your face is so wonderfully like one I once knew — and loved."

As he spoke the last words his voice sank almost to a whisper, while his eyes with a singular eagerness were fixed on mine. I had a feeling that much hung upon my reply, though just what revelation it might lead to, curiously perhaps, did not occur to me.

"Yes," I said, "I have been told by my father that I have my mother's looks. She was a Paduan, and her maiden name was Bianca Gambacorta."

"I might have known it!" he cried, "I might have known it! The same curve of the brows, the same expression about the mouth, the same nose and chin; and then the eyes!" He came toward me with hands outstretched.

"Luigi," he said, — "I remember that we heard you were called Luigi, — welcome to your mother's home!"

How strange it all seemed to me a few hours later, and yet how fortunate! Indeed, I blessed the thieves who had way-laid and robbed me, for through them I had found my cousin. The letter which I had entrusted to the care of his steward had never reached him, having been lost in transmission, and but for what appeared the intervention of fate years might have elapsed before we encountered each other. Now Alberto Gambacorta seemed like an old friend. He had heard the story of my life with rapt attention, and I related everything to him without reserve. More than once when I mentioned my father's name a cloud passed over his kindly face, and when I told him of the cause of my quitting home he sprang up in unmistak-able pain and agitation. It was some mo-ments before he regained his self-control, but once having mastered his anger, there was no recurrence of the strong passion that had moved him.

When I had finished speaking he sat for a long time in thought, his eyes averted. Finally he raised his head.

"There are but two of us, Luigi," he said. "Why should we live apart?

Will you not, after a little, make this house your home? I realize that there are certain reasons for your returning to Milan, but will you not promise me that as soon as may be you will come back to this roof for an abiding-place? It was here that your mother spent her early happy days, and while it is mine now, it is the same as yours, for yours it will one day be."

"The promise you ask," I answered, "is most gladly given. I have told you that I have begun to distrust the Visconti, and would willingly quit his service. This already seems to me like home. Even now I would remain were it not for—" here I hesitated.

"I think I understand," my cousin said. "You would make report to your master, and give to him duly your reasons for quitting his employ; you would have a last interview with your father; and you would see if you cannot find some trace of the whereabouts of a certain maiden. Am I not right?"

"In the main you are. But why

should I seek my father's presence if I cannot force him to retract his base imputations ? "

" I feel that you will be able to do this when you have heard the story of my life and that of your mother, though perchance then you will wish to retract your promise to return to Padua."

With these words my cousin left me to rest (for my head had times of throbbing painfully) and to meditate upon his parting speech, together with the strange chance which had brought me under the roof where my mother had spent her maidenhood. It was not until we sat at dinner over a confection of prunes and the last of a flask of lacrima Christi that he turned back for me the leaves of the book of the past. I saw by his manner that it was an ordeal to him, — this laying bare of a life full of painful memories, — and from first to last I did not once break in upon his narrative.

" You have doubtless heard, Luigi," he began, " that your mother was reared by an uncle and aunt, my father and mother.

They took charge of her almost from infancy, for your grandparents were carried off by the plague when Bianca was but three. I was five years of age when she came into the family, and we grew up together like brother and sister. I never thought of her, or looked upon her, in other than a brotherly way until I chanced one day to overhear some words spoken to my father. 'Your niece has grown to be the very flower of Paduan maids,' the speaker said. 'He will be a fortunate man who wears such a flower upon his breast.' From that hour I was changed, nor was Bianca slow to note the difference in me, and to divine the cause. How many, many times have I wished in these lonely later years that mine had been a more troubled wooing! That Bianca and I should marry was the desire nearest my father's and mother's heart, and my cousin confessed, after I had told her of my love, that her affection for me had long ceased to be sisterly. Thus was my path strewn with roses, not an obstacle, not a hinder-ance, thrown in my way; everything made smooth for me, so that I did not realize the inestimable boon I had won.

"Despite the fact that my parents so earnestly desired the match, they insisted that we should wait a year before we set the wedding day. Doubtless they thought this provision wise and just, for we were both young. Could they have looked into the future, I am sure they would not have decreed the delay. Before six months had gone by, chance led me into evil company — companionship which I should have shunned, but which I courted instead. Your mother's influence, my parents' entreaties, neither sufficed to make me see whither my course was leading me. I was a senseless fool, blind to the magnitude of my folly. At last the time came when the day for our wedding was to be set. The year of probation had passed. Bianca met me in the presence of my parents. I can see this moment how sad she looked, and yet how resolute. There was a loving appeal in her eyes as she spoke; for strangely, through all, her heart remained true to me. 'Alberto,' she said, 'there must be another year of waiting if you would claim me for your wife, and'—her voice broke—'and you must go away for a time. Perhaps when you come back you will be like your old self once more. Then, oh, then—' but her sobs choked her, and I turned from her to my father and mother in amazement, consternation, and shame. Of this—contemptible wretch that I had been!—I never dreamed.

"I strove to protest, but despite my protestations and promises my mother led Bianca from the room, and I was left face to face with my father. 'You go, sir, on the morrow,' he said icily, 'not to a place where you will be free from temptations, but where they will be multiplied an hundred fold—to the city of Constantinople, the seat of the most corrupt court in Europe. You will bear letters to one whom I once knew well, a man who by birth and place will be able to give you a chance to see every side of the varied life of the great Eastern metropolis. If you rise from the slough into which you have fallen, and prove worthy of the blood that flows in your veins, all will be well; but otherwise you need never hope to call wife the pure girl whose heart you have so cruelly torn.'

" Thus was I rudely jarred into a realization that I had undermined my house of happiness. I put aside all my follies, and when, after an absence of eight months, I returned to Padua I had nothing to look back upon with regret during the period of my foreign sojourn, despite the fact that I had much of the time been thrown with the gay and dissolute youth of a decadent empire. But I found that a new and wholly unforeseen element had been introduced into my home life during my tarry in Constantinople. This was in the person of Giovanni della Verria, your father, who had come to listen to the lectures of a noted doctor of jurisprudence, then resident at the University of Padua. The Pavian bore with him letters to my father and mother, and had grown to be a frequent and welcome visitor at our house. He had attracted Bianca by his distinguished address and by the brilliancy of his acquirements, and when I arrived I found the two upon a very friendly footing, which I was not slow to discover meant something more than friendship on his part. With Bianca's greeting and manner toward me for some weeks after my home-coming I could find no fault; and though your father was a frequent guest, I felt so secure in my cousin's affection that his noticeable admiration for her aroused in me no jealousy.

"A month before the time when our wedding day was finally to be set, it came into your mother's mind, so I afterward learned, that she would submit me to a final test. I cannot wonder, when I consider my shortcomings, and yet I know she afterward lamented her action with many bitter tears. It was wholly unfair to your father, it was unjust to me, it was beneath her true and womanly nature. Had she paused to consider, I am sure her sober second thought would have counselled her against playing with the affections, even allowing that her main purpose was in a sense worthy.

"When I saw Bianca show Giovanni della Verria marked favors I could not at first believe my senses. 'She is only trying me,' I said to myself, when I recovered from my first surprise, which was the truth. 'He knows of our betrothal,' I thought, 'and if he wishes to play the moth and singe his wings at the candle, it is no affair of mine.' No harm would have resulted had I followed out my resolution to hold my peace, but in an untoward hour I ventured to ask my cousin if she had not acted her comedy long enough. Provoked that I should see through her motives, she pretended not to understand me, and I, suddenly conceiving that I might after all be mistaken, spoke a few hasty words of reproach, whereupon she flashed out upon me, 'What are you, sir, that you dare to reproach me?' — this with a fine scorn of which I did not dream her capable. Now although there was much justice in her retort, there had been a sort of understanding between us that there was to be no reference to things by-gone, so I was deeply hurt. I replied hotly, just what I never could recall, nor do I know what she said, save that there was some reference to the necessity of my taking another journey. It was with this in mind that I rushed from her presence, and before the sun set that night I was on my way to Germany.

"I will not trouble you with my reflections, nor will I dwell upon her regrets when she found she had actually driven me away. Messengers were despatched to recall me, but their search for me was vain. I had met with a severe accident in one of the mountain passes, and lay for weeks in a peasant's hut unable to move, caring little whether I was living or dead. Somehow a rumor reached Padua that I had indeed been killed, and as months passed and nothing was heard from me, the report was accepted as truth.

" A year slipped away before I set my face toward home. Chance led me to the chief city of a small German principality to whose master I was able to be of some

little use with my sword. That in Padua
I should be considered dead did not occur
to me, and I still thought of Bianca with
alternate hope and fear. But return I
would not until I could feel that I was in
every respect the master of myself.

"Alas, the cruel shock of my home-
coming! I found my father and mother
broken with grief at my supposed end, and
my cousin, she of whom I had dreamed of
one day making myself worthy, two
months married to Giovanni della Verria.
She had vehemently resented the idea at
first in her grief over my death, of which
she accused herself of being the cause, but
being assiduously importuned by your
father, and urged by my parents, who,
now that they thought me no longer living,
were anxious about her future, she finally
consented.

"There was naught for me to do but
to face the inevitable, but the struggle
cost me many a sleepless night, many a
day of mental misery. Then a letter
which was not meant for my eyes fell
into my hands, and I knew that Bianca

N

was not happy in her new life.   My
fancied mastery over myself was gone.
Madman that I was, I resolved to see her.
At my own request she had not yet been
told of my return as it were from the
dead, and I did not pause to think what
effect my unexpected appearance might
have upon her.   Concealing my intention
from my parents, I set out for Pavia.   Ar-
riving there, I made such changes in my
appearance as would prevent Giovanni
della Verria from recognizing me should
I meet him upon the street, and then
started forth to find his residence.   This
was not difficult, but to gain an interview
alone with Bianca was quite another matter.   I watched the entrance for the
greater part of a day without avail until
the fact that I was being regarded curiously by passers-by bade me be cautious.
Never once did I take into account that
I could do nothing for Bianca, that my
presence might not only prove an embarrassment but might actually add to her
unhappiness. No, I was so consumed
with the idea that I must see her again,

that I must somehow comfort her, that I did not consider the possible consequences of making my presence known.

"Late in the day I saw your father emerge from the house, and not long afterward a girl came forth whom I fancied must be Bianca's maid. I followed her, and when she had gone a little distance, stopped her and inquired if she served the Signora della Verria. Receiving an affirmative reply, I drew a ring from my finger which my cousin had once given me, and bade the girl, as soon as opportunity offered, put it into her mistress' hand, and say to her that the wearer of the ring sought an interview with her. The maid seemed much frightened at first, but finally consented to do as I wished. It was agreed that I should await her near a certain street corner at the same hour on the following day. 'My master always goes forth to the promenade at this time,' she said.

"The girl was prompt to keep her appointment. Before she could speak I questioned her eagerly. 'What said your mistress?' I asked. 'Ah, Signore,' she replied, 'I thought the dear lady had fallen into a swoon, she gave such a cry, and dropped back so faint, when I put the ring into her hand. She has not been herself since.' 'But when am I to see her?' I cried. 'Now,' said the maid, looking about her apprehensively, as though she feared some one, 'at once; you are to come with me. The time may be short.'

"My head was in a whirl as I followed her, scarcely looking whither she led. I had my wits sufficiently about me, however, to note that it was not the main entrance by which we gained access to the house. Swiftly and silently we threaded several passages, ascended a flight of stairs, and then I found myself in a small room where I recognized the touch of Bianca's hands. The maid left me hurriedly, and an instant later your mother entered. Ah, Luigi, the emotions I read upon her beautiful face!— love, joy, sorrow, fear, and a certain something I had not seen before, and could not at the moment fathom. When I saw her, for the first time I realized the unwisdom of my course. I knew in a flash that it was only an added weight of regret and unhappiness that my coming was likely to bring to her. All she could say was to reiterate my name, a sound that floats down through the years to me sweeter than any mortal music. While I was soothing her, and kissing her fondly, she suddenly started back from me, as though she had dreamed and was awaking to a painful reality.

" 'You must go, Alberto,' she said earnestly, but sadly, 'and go at once. I ought never to have consented to see you at all, but oh, I could not refuse when it seemed to me as though you had risen from the grave. Some time in our old home we may meet again, but not here. No good could come of it. My husband is so jealous, so suspicious, though why, God knows. I suppose it is my punishment for striving to arouse jealousy in you.'

" I cried out against her entertaining

such a feeling, but she made no reply save to urge me to leave her. Seeing that I still hesitated, she exclaimed: 'Heaven knows what would happen should he find you here! Go for my sake, Alberto, and that of my child!' Scarcely had this wholly unexpected and touching appeal fallen from her lips when the maid rushed in. 'The Signore!' she cried in terror. There was no time for concealment, for in another instant Giovanni della Verria stood in the doorway. The maid had been watching for his return by the front entrance, and had heard his steps from the opposite approach when too late to give any warning save the cry which announced his presence. Pausing upon the threshold, he looked darkly from Bianca to me, whom he did not recognize.

"'So, Signora,' he said, 'I see that you have a lover. With him I will reckon first, and then, my lady, I will return and reckon with you.' He drew his sword and waved to me to follow him. 'Signor della Verria,' I cried, thinking to make some sort of an explanation, but he gave no heed to me. I cast a last glance at Bianca, who was gazing stonily at the door through which her husband had disappeared, then I strode after him. In the large reception-room below he turned and faced me. Now he saw who I was, and grew only the more enraged. He would listen to no word, and I speedily realized that if I valued my life I must defend myself. He closed and fastened the doors, and soon the room rang with the clash of our weapons.

"However your father may have changed in later years, he then knew well the use of the sword, but his rage was his undoing. Before five minutes had passed I had run him through the shoulder and disarmed him. 'Hark you,' I said to him as he stood biting his lip in impotent anger and pain, 'your wife is as innocent of the foul slander you put upon her as the veriest babe in arms.' 'I do not believe it,' he muttered. 'It is true,' I cried, 'on my oath.' Still I saw that he did not believe me. 'It came to my knowledge,' I said, 'that she was unhappy, and in the memory of my old love for her I foolishly hastened here, and as foolishly contrived to gain her presence. What blame there is, is mine. Now before I go out from your sight, I trust forever, you shall swear in Jesus' name and that of the holy Virgin that no harm shall come to my cousin through your hand or your agency. Down on your knees.' My sword point was at his throat, and he read death in my eyes if he refused. Slowly he went down upon the floor, repeated the oath, and made the sign of the cross as I bade. There was all the hate of hell in the look he gave me when he had uttered the words. 'If you break your oath,' I exclaimed, as I turned to leave him, 'may your soul rot in torment!' As I passed out of the room he fell over in a dead faint. 'Your master needs your attention in the reception-hall,' I said to a servant I met in the courtyard. Then I hastened out into the street, and in half an hour had turned my back on Pavia.

"You may blame me, Luigi, if you

will, but you cannot condemn me more severely than I have condemned myself through all these years. Since my father's and my mother's death, which followed soon upon that of your mother, I have been a wanderer on the face of the earth, driven up and down the world by my regretful memories, almost my only comfort being the knowledge that after your birth your mother's life became more bearable, for whatever your father may have felt in his heart, he kept his oath. Never until to-day has it seemed to me that I could tarry long in one spot, but now that you have heard my story, if you still feel that you can return to Padua and to a life beneath this roof, it will be a joy to me to abide here and do what I can to make you contented and happy, and should you by any chance bring another, she shall be more than welcome for your mother's sake."

He regarded me with unmistakable anxiety as he finished, as though he feared I would turn my back upon him for the suffering and sorrow he had brought into

my mother's life, but it was with no sense
of resentment that I had listened to the
recital of the history of his past, but rather
one of pity; for looking into the face of
the man, I could but see the mirror of a
true and noble heart, that had long and
fondly cherished the deepest love for her for
whom he had so grieved, and upon whom
he had brought such trouble.   All the love
and hate, the passion and the pain, of the
bygone years had tempered my cousin's
soul as doth the white fire the steel; for
when I had unhesitatingly renewed my
promise to him, he spoke in extenuating
terms of my father's conduct, praising his
remarkable parts, saying that all mankind
had their failings, pointing out how grievous a misfortune it is to be the possessor
of an ungovernably suspicious and jealous
temperament.

When I parted from Alberto Gambacorta, and mounted Hawkwood in the
fresh air of the early spring morning, it
was with a happier heart than had beat in
my breast for many a long day.   I had
found a real home, and one whom I could

love; the old bitterness against my father had in a measure died from my thoughts; and the image of Angela Canaro rose before me with beguiling and beckoning eyes.

Chapter XIII

The Affair of the Via San Lorenzo

ON the last day of my return journey to Milan, Hawkwood fell so lame that it was hard upon dusk ere I rode through the gates of the city. My first care was to see my steed properly attended to; this done, I repaired to the lodgings I had recently taken, with my master's permission, in a small street leading from the piazza where the palace stood. I had for some time been eager to transfer my belongings from my contracted quarters in the palace, but had only lately effected my desire.

While the good housewife who presided over my new abode was filling my ears with the public gossip, I fell to wondering whether I had best report to my master that night or wait until the morrow.   That he would be surprised at my determination to quit his service I felt sure, and I had no notion how he would take it.   Finally I came to the conclusion that I should sleep better if I had the whole matter off my mind; accordingly, when I had changed my soiled riding-garb, I took a hasty dinner, and sallied forth in the direction of the palace.   There was still a faint trace of the golden afterglow in the sky when I reached the piazza, and the place was gay with strolling pleasurers, fair ladies, some of whom were not at all anxious to conceal their faces behind their masks, ogling gallants who ruffled it as gamely as a company of cocks with fine feathers, a plentiful sprinkling of sedate merchants with their wives, together with soldiers, and rogues of both sexes.

I picked my way leisurely through the chattering throng until presently I drew near the palace gateway.   As I approached, two of the city's fashionable young bloods brushed past me, evidently bent upon following out some light affair of the heart.

One of them dropped his mask as he hurried by, and such was his haste that he did not stop to pick it from the pavement. I gazed at the bit of black folly with its staring eye-holes, and then, moved by I know not what impulse, stooped and lifted it. Even as I looked, its owner was lost to view in the crowd, and with the mask in my hand I resumed my way. Scarcely had I taken half a dozen steps, however, before I saw a man issue from the palace courtyard who staggered like one in a drunken fit. Amazement halted me, and held me riveted in my tracks, for the man was Vincenzo Canaro.

As he came on, I realized that his eyes were fixed and that he observed nothing. His face was not that of a man overcome by the fumes of wine, but rather that of one whose brain was undergoing some tense strain. Despair was written upon every feature, and a great compassion for him seized me. My first impulse was to rush forward and speak to him, but it suddenly came to me that in all probability he would not recognize me, and that in his present state I should doubtless be rudely repulsed. As he passed me, he appeared to recover himself a little and glanced about as though to assure himself of his whereabouts. His eyes fell upon me, but there was no gleam of recognition in them.

My resolve was now swiftly taken. I would follow him, discover his abode, and on the morrow make myself known. It might be that in some way I could be of service; for that Signor Canaro was in deep trouble I felt confident, and I shrewdly suspected that his trouble emanated from my master. That my wish to discover the abode of the Brescian noble was solely because of my desire to offer him my aid I will not assert. In this matter I did not deceive myself. But the fact that I had another end in view did not lessen the sincerity of my intention to be of assistance to him.

Slipping on the mask, the possession of which now struck me as being a rare bit of good fortune, and drawing about me my cloak, which I had thrown over my arm, I hugged the wall, following a score of paces in the rear of the dejected man. He looked neither to the right nor to the left, and as far as his observing me was concerned, I might have hung close upon his heels and he never have been the wiser. At first I encountered a goodly number of people moving in the direction of the piazza, but presently, drawing away from the centre of the city, there was but little life in the streets, and it was only at corners, or before wine-shops, that I met more than a solitary loiterer. Apparently no one gave heed to me, but if any one did bestow a thought upon me, it was doubtless to surmise that I was an enamoured gallant, speeding to keep an evening tryst.

At length I found myself in the Via San Lorenzo. Although not especially familiar with the quarter of the city into which Signor Canaro was leading me, I recognized this street from the proximity of the church of the same name whose dome loomed large through the fast-thickening dusk. Quickening my pace a trifle, lest the object of my quest should disappear in some cross-thoroughfare and leave me in doubt as to which house he had entered, I was but a short distance behind him when he reached the first of the sixteen Corinthian columns that remain to tell of the stateliness of the baths with which the Emperor Maximian adorned Roman Mediolanum. Not even one lone loiterer was in view. High in the window of an adjacent dwelling a single, feeble taper flared, the only sign of life. The spot was singularly solitary considering the hour.

As Signor Canaro reached a point abreast of the last column I was stealing toward the first, intending to pass in the rear of the colonnade, when three men leaped noiselessly from their concealment behind the pillars and flung themselves upon the unsuspecting Brescian, bearing him to the earth. The poor man gave a loud cry as he fell, and that cry spurred me to instant action. Whipping out my sword, I dashed upon his assailants, running one of them through the groin, as he rose to meet me, and thrusting violently at the second, who strove to entangle me in his cloak. By this time the third had his weapon out, and I was horrified to see him, as Signor Canaro strove to regain his feet, lunge viciously at the unfortunate man, who staggered and sank back. Thinking him disposed of, the swordsman sprang at me. Like myself he was masked, and so fierce and furious was his sword-play, that in the dim light I was hard put to it to save my skin from a pinking. While the caitiff with the cloak was assisting his wounded companion, the man in the mask and I hacked and hewed at one another till the sparks danced about us like swamp-fires, and the street echoed with our violent cuts and parries. It was haphazard fencing, sheer guess-work oftentimes, but each seemed to know instinctively what the other would attempt, and so we slashed, while lights grew in the few windows that looked upon this portion of the thoroughfare, and cries of " murder " and shouts for the watchman swelled about our ears.

I wondered at the persistence of my opponent, now that the neighborhood was so aroused ; in fact, I could not understand why he assaulted me at all, his end being apparently achieved in the blow he struck Signor Canaro, who had not moved since he received the stroke. The dress of my antagonist gave me no clew to his identity, but there was something about his movements that struck me as familiar, though I could by no means say where I had met him at fence before. Now there came the sound of nearing footsteps, and making a final desperate lunge which caused me to fall back a step, he caught up my cloak, which had fallen upon the ground between us, and disappeared in a black alley whither I knew it was futile to follow him. His companions had made good their escape during our encounter, and so when those whose footfalls I had heard arrived, they found me bending over the body of the prostrate nobleman, endeavoring to discover if there were still any signs of life left in him. Life there was, though his breast was soaked with blood, and when the light of a lantern was flashed into his eyes he opened them with a dazed and painful look.

" Whither shall we bear you, Signore ? " said I.

And he had just strength enough to tell me, lapsing again, immediately afterward, into unconsciousness.

My guardsman's uniform gave me authority among those who had gathered about us, — worthy citizens of the upper class they were, all of them ; so bidding one go in search of a reputable leech, with the assistance of the others I bore Signor Canaro toward the house he had indicated, which was situated in the street just beyond the church of San Lorenzo.

We found the portal of the dwelling ajar, and from it two women were peering into the night.   As we halted, one of them, whom I recognized with a quickened beat of the heart, sprang from the doorway and darted in among us.   More lovely than ever she seemed to me, in her simple gown and loosely bound hair, about which the flickering light played like a halo.

" Bidding one go in search of a reputable leech." — Page 196

She gazed into her father's face, which wore the pallor of apparent death, gave a low moan, and would have fallen had a kindly hand not lent her support.

"Courage, Signorina," said he who had assisted her; "there is hope. He has but fainted. A leech will be here presently, and in the meantime do you show us where we may lay him."

These words restored her to herself in a measure, and calling to her woman, who was still standing helplessly in the doorway, she bade her lead the way. After we had laid Signor Canaro upon a couch and forced a few drops of wine down his throat, the color began to creep back into his cheeks, and presently he opened his eyes. When he saw his daughter bending over him, he smiled, and a look of contentment spread over his features, but he did not try to speak. All save two of us now retired from the apartment. I should have slipped away, but it seemed desirable that some one should remain to be of use should the surgeon require assistance; and inasmuch as I had been the only witness to the assault upon Signor Canaro, it was insisted that I should be one of those to stay.

An aged man-servant now slipped in and stood by one side of the bed, while on the other side knelt the daughter of the wounded man. A striking picture it was, and one that moved me strongly to compassion. The hangings of the bed threw heavy shadows over the form out-stretched upon it, and had it not been for the sound of labored breathing one would have said that Death was present in the room. Indeed, his presence did seem to be there. It was as though in pity for the stricken maiden he was delaying a little space before claiming his own.

After a time we heard the door open below, there were steps upon the stair, and then the surgeon entered. He was a man of skill and worked rapidly, and such was his personality that with his coming the gloom was suddenly dispelled, the tense strain relaxed. We found ourselves of little aid, and so kept in the background.

"There is no danger," we heard him say at length to Signorina Canaro. "Loss of blood and the shock have caused this prostration. A bone turned the blade, and saved his life, Signorina."

He asked no questions, and I believe up to this point, so great had been her anxiety, the thought of how it had happened had not entered the mind of Angela Canaro. Now, however, that her fears were relieved, the natural wish to know how her father had received his wound became uppermost, and for the first time she turned to us with expressions of gratitude. Indeed, until now she had given no heed to our presence, so great had been her solicitude for her father.

"I trust you will pardon me, gentlemen," she said, as she approached us, "for not expressing my gratitude for your kindness before, but —" she paused, and cast her eyes toward the bed, while a sob rose in her throat.

"Think not of thanking us, Signorina," said my companion. "We understand, and now that we are no longer needed we will not further intrude upon you."

He passed toward the doorway, and I was about to follow when she said, —

" But can you not tell me how my father came to be hurt ? "

" This gentleman knows more of the matter than I," answered the man, and continued on his way as though anxious to be gone.

Signorina Canaro now turned toward me, and for the first time, I think, had a fair view of my face, for she gave a little start, and a gleam of half recognition flashed in her dark eyes.

" Have I not seen you before ? " she said.   " Are you not the Signor della Verria ? "

" Yes, Signorina," said I.

Impulsively she grasped my hand, and at her words I felt a new energy, a sense of power I had not known before thrill through me.

" God has sent you to us, Signore," said she.   " My father is in some great trouble which he will not confide to me, and is in sore want of a friend.   I have never forgotten some words of yours spoken at our home in Brescia when you bade us adieu. You offered me the protection of your sword should the time ever come when I needed a third defender. That was in the presence of my father and Signor Ardotti, the poor brave Signor Ardotti who is now dead, as mayhap you know. It is not for myself that I would now ask the redemption of that promise, but for my father, Signore."

Ah, the sweet pleading earnestness with which she said these words! What man with a drop of ardor in his veins could have withstood them? For me, who had long fostered in my mind the fondest and the fairest thoughts of her, it was difficult not to reply with too great warmth. Yet restrain myself as I would, it was impossible for me to repress my devotion both in tone and speech.

"Believe me, Signorina," I exclaimed, "that offer was not lightly made, and for you or for your father I am as ready to strike now as I was then."

The look of relief that crossed her face as I spoke did not escape me, and thereat still more was I elated. It mattered little to me at that moment what unknown dangers I might be called upon to encounter, what subtle and hidden foes I might be forced to combat, in behalf of Signor Canaro and his daughter. I felt equal to coping with and overcoming them all.

At Signorina Canaro's request I now related to her how her father came by his wound, taking care not to state that I had followed him from the piazza, but leaving her to infer rather that I had been a chance witness of the assault.

"How much are we already indebted to you!" she cried.

The leech now summoned her, wishing to give her some instructions in regard to the care of her father, and assuring her that I would without fail call in the morning to inquire after the invalid and to see if I could not be of some service, I took my leave, translating her warm expressions of gratitude into something sweeter as I passed along the street.

Through the open door of the church

of San Lorenzo there came the faint glimmer of tapers, and while I confess that I commonly have more faith in the virtue of a strong right arm than in the interposition of the saints, I slipped into the sacred edifice, and made a supplication and a vow before the holy shrine during the course of which the name Angela was more than once devoutly whispered.

Chapter XIV

I have Some Last Words with my Father

I PRESENTED myself in good time at the palace the next morning, only to learn that my master was indisposed and would probably see no one that day. Reporting to the captain of the guard, I requested leave of absence until night. This was really but a matter of form, and my wish was readily granted; for, as I have before indicated, I was only nominally under the captain's authority, receiving nearly all my orders from my master himself.

After hearing that the Visconti would that day receive no one, I immediately decided that I would utilize the hours that might otherwise hang heavily, by making an excursion to Pavia, and getting off my mind the interview with my father. Then, at the first opportunity, I would resign my position, and feel free to devote myself to the cause of Signor and Angela Canaro. Something told me that as a lieutenant of Gian Galeazzo's palace guard I was scarcely in a position to be of the most efficient service to the unfortunate Brescian and his daughter. I surmised that Signor Canaro had come to Milan at the suggestion, if not at the command, of my master, and I believed that the Visconti was in some way responsible for the trouble of which Angela Canaro had spoken the night before. Indeed, I had begun to think that the cowardly attack in the Via San Lorenzo was something of his instigation. Six months earlier it would not have occurred to me to suspect him of such baseness, but my eyes had been gradually opened to what lay behind that calm, calculating, and crafty exterior.

Granted that my suspicions were true, how could I, single-handed, hope to effect anything against his shrewdness and power? Should I not, if it became known that I was acting the meddler, endanger my own safety ? In the enthusiasm of youth and love these things I did not pause to consider. I had a vision of Angela Canaro safe in Padua at my cousin's house (which he had bidden me regard also mine), and this for the time being was enough to lift me above earth. How this seemingly miraculous transfer was to be brought about had, just then, no place in my thoughts. Ah, the confidence that the magic stirring of love inspires in the heart of youth! Yet who shall say that many wondrous things are not wrought thereby ?

Before making any preparations for my Pavian pilgrimage I hastened to the abode of the wounded Brescian, and was rejoiced to hear that he had wonderfully recovered.

"He insists upon seeing you," said Signorina Canaro, anxiously ; "for I told him to whom he was indebted for his rescue, and promised I would bring you to him when you came, fearing to refuse would excite him and do him more harm than a few moments' talk with you."

When I entered the presence of Signor Canaro, I could scarcely believe I saw before me the same man upon whom I had looked the night previous and wondered if he had an hour's hold on life. True, there was something feverish in the eagerness with which he greeted me, and I feared that the strength he seemed to show might be born of excitement, but there was no trace of unnatural heat in the hand which he placed in mine, and I was forced to conclude either that his recuperative powers were remarkable, or that there was magic in the leech's art.

After he had expressed his gratitude in feeling terms for the service which I had rendered him, he made a little sign to his daughter, who at once withdrew. As I seated myself by the bedside of the wounded man, I was conscious that he was concentrating upon me his most searching gaze as though he would penetrate the workings of my mind and read my thoughts.

"Signor della Verria," he said at length, "though I know little of you, I believe you to be a man of honor. My daughter has told me of your offer of last night, and I recall your chivalrous words spoken some time since in Brescia. I would fain trust in you, for God knows I need some one in whom to trust, but there is one thing that makes me hesitate to do so."

He paused before speaking further, letting his eyes rest with the same eager intentness upon my face.

" Perhaps if I knew why you hesitate," said I, " I might be able to persuade you that you do so without reason."

He reflected for an instant, then he spoke with sharp decision.

" I will tell you," he said. " You serve Gian Galeazzo Visconti, and if you serve him honestly, I do not see how you can aid my daughter and myself."

" That fact need have no weight with you," I answered; " for it is my intention, and has been since my visit to Padua, to resign my position under the Visconti at the first opportunity. I sought him this morning for that purpose, but found him indisposed."

A gleam of something more than satisfaction passed over Signor Canaro's face.

" Perhaps you are beginning to understand the character of the master whom you serve," he said.

" I am," I replied.

" I have not the strength this morning," he said, now speaking rapidly, " to explain to you my position, but I am in danger of losing my freedom if not my life, and my daughter's safety is involved in mine. It is for her sake that I am consumed with anxiety, it is for her sake that I am forced to beg aid from you, almost a stranger, for in this whole city there is not one man whom I can call friend."

" You would leave Milan ? " I asked. " Whither would you go ? "

" Anywhere ! anywhere ! " he cried, " to escape from the coils of that viper, Gian Galeazzo Visconti.

It was the first time I had heard the term "viper" applied to my master, and there is small wonder that I started at the sound of it.

"His arms are well chosen," said Signor Canaro, noticing my involuntary movement.

"You may count upon my aid," I said, rising, for I saw that he was becoming over-excited and fatigued.

"But the danger to yourself, bethink you of that! Should our attempt be circumvented, and your present master discover your part in it, you might be involved in our ruin. I would have you count the possible cost."

"I am willing to risk it, and I have a friend on whose advice I can depend, if not upon his assistance." My thought flew to Hartzheim as I said this.

"Then we must haste, else it will be too late."

"I will come again this evening," I said. "It will not do for us to talk further now."

As I was seeking the street I encountered the Signorina. Her eyes were full of anxiety, and I stopped to give her a reassuring word. The smile which I had in return made bright my journey to

Pavia, which I took beneath a lowering sky.

Hawkwood was still a trifle lame, but I had no difficulty in obtaining a mount, and as the new bell in Santa Maria del Carmine was clanging the hour of noon I rode up in front of a little inn called the Golden Bull, where I had had many an excellent supper. It was good to see again the rubicund face of "mine host," Tommaso, and to hear his cheery greeting. It was good, too, to look upon the familiar streets and well-known countenances of the townsfolk, and to listen to their pleasant salutations. Some of the burghers made much of me, for I had grown to be a man of importance in their eyes, now that I had followed Gian Galeazzo to Milan. All this warmed my heart so that I half forgot my errand. My affection toward my birthplace and the home of my youth was quickened, and there crept a regret into my thoughts that fate was leading my steps into far-away paths.

Not until the stroke of mid-afternoon

did I return to a realization of my purpose. I knew by this time that my father would have finished his siesta, and would, unless his habits had strangely changed, be poring over some Latin parchment in his library. Bidding the friends with whom I chanced to be visiting adieu, for the first time in many a long month I set my face toward the house I had once called home. I was conscious of a queer sensation in my throat as I turned into the oft-trod street, every stone of which it seemed to me I knew. There was none of the burning bitterness in my breast that had rankled there when I had fled my father's presence. I found it difficult to analyze my feeling toward him, but it was one of compassion rather than of anger. It was not that I resented any the less deeply the wrong which he had done my mother, but that I comprehended, as I did not before, the workings of the suspicious and unhappy nature that made possible such a wrong.

I had come with no reproaches, no upbraidings. I looked upon the approaching interview as a plain matter of duty. I was determined that he should hear my cousin's story, and I would relate it to him dispassionately. Then, I felt that it was due to him that he should know my plans for the future. I had kept him in the dark long enough. There were certain rights of inheritance of which he could not deprive me, even should he choose to do so, but these, save what was mine from my mother, it was my purpose to renounce.

As I turned into the courtyard I almost ran into a tall, slender youth who was passing out. We stared at one another an instant before there was any recognition. The youth was my half-brother, Rinaldo, marvellously changed in stature since I had last put eyes on him.

"Why, it's Luigi!" he cried, in a way that surprised me; for our relations in the past had been none of the pleasantest, owing, I had always fancied, to his mother's influence rather than to any inherent dislike of me on the boy's part. Now he seemed actually glad to see me, kissing me with real cordiality upon the cheeks, then stepping back and gazing at my accoutrement.

"How fine you look!" exclaimed he. "It must be a grand thing to be a soldier. Will you not help me to be one, Luigi?"

"You a soldier, Rinaldo!" cried I, in amazement.

"Yes," said he, "why not? You are one. Oh!" he exclaimed, with a sudden change of tone, "you are thinking of what father would say!"

He had hit it fairly. Of that I was thinking. When my father had taken my liking for arms so sorely to heart, what would he say indeed should he find Rinaldo's thoughts (Rinaldo who was the very apple of his eye) bent in the same direction?

"He can't say anything," exclaimed my half-brother, as though something had all at once occurred to him, "for he is sick in bed, and has been these two months. I suppose you've come to see him; but you can't, for the mother won't let you."

"Father sick in bed these two months!" cried I, in astonishment. "What ails him?"

"The doctors say it is a gouty rheum." We had now turned across the courtyard, and were approaching the stairway. Up this we passed together, I replying to Rinaldo's questions in haphazard fashion, only half realizing what he was asking me. That an illness should overtake my father was something that had never entered my head. He had always seemed a man beyond the touch of ailment. Never in my recollection could I recall hearing him complain of feeling ill. Could it be, now that I had come to speak with him for what might be the last time, that I was to be prevented because he lay helpless on a sick-bed, and a woman who had always thwarted my wishes whenever it lay in her power stood in the way? "No," I said to myself; "see him I will, if I have to force myself into his presence."

As Rinaldo and I entered the apartment from which the bedchamber where my father was lying opened, a voice from the inner room which I recognized as that of my step-mother called, —

" Who is there ? "

I had no wish to see my father in her presence, so I did not at once step forward, neither did I speak, fearing if she heard my voice the door would be closed in my face.   Rinaldo was also silent, taking the cue from me.   Presently I heard her rise and approach the entrance.   Bidding my step-brother stand where he was near the centre of the room, I slipped into a corner, thinking to be for an instant unobserved, and knowing that if I could but once get between her and the doorway my purpose would be achieved.

It all chanced as I hoped.   Seeing Rinaldo, she walked toward him, asking him what he desired, while I sprang in behind her, caught the door handle, swung the panelled barrier shut, set my back to it and faced her before she was fully aware what had taken place.   When she realized how easily she had been circumvented, she turned upon me with all the rage of a

foiled tigress. Her eyes, which were usually large and cold and gray, contracted
on a sudden, and became like glistening
points of fire. Her lips were so tightly
drawn that the white points of her teeth
showed beneath them.

"How dare you? how dare you?" she
demanded. "Stand aside, and let me go
to my husband. I had hoped, as he had,
that we should never look upon your
ungrateful face again. Get you gone to
your brawlers and your bravos!"

She advanced as though she would
attempt to seize hold of me and force me
from the position I had taken, but I did
not cow before her anger; and though she
was a large woman and strong, I had no
fear that she really intended to pit her
strength against mine.

"Signora," I said to her calmly, "I
have come hither to see my father, and
see him I will, nor can any word or act of
yours prevent me. I regret that I am
compelled to take just this means to
achieve my end, but past experience has
taught me that there is no other way."

"You are insulting, basely insulting!" cried she, in a towering rage.

"But, mother," Rinaldo interposed, "has he not a right to see father?"

"You fool," his mother replied, seeking some one on whom to vent her anger, "it is you who have brought him here, who have allowed him to make his way to this room, to force himself into his father's presence — his father whose every wish he has disregarded, whose life he has embittered, and whose sick-bed he would now unfeelingly intrude upon!"

This outburst seemed to have small effect upon Rinaldo, and I could but reflect that the boy had freed himself in a remarkable manner from the leading-strings since my departure from home.

"Signora," said I, "it seems to me that you waste words. I have no desire for a long interview with my father, but I tell you once for all, see him I will. If you return to this place at the end of three-quarters of an hour, you will find me gone, and I can promise you that if we ever meet again that meeting will not be one of my seeking."

Slowly she removed her gaze from my face, a gaze in which the most intense hatred was still dominant. Deliberately she turned, and as deliberately walked from the apartment, bidding Rinaldo follow her. Throwing me a look in which amusement and resignation were mingled, he went out after her.

I regretted the necessity of this scene, but regrets were useless. Never could I have persuaded my step-mother that I had not returned to demand my rights as the eldest son and heir of the house. It was her jealousy of my position that aroused in her such hatred and antagonism. Doubtless since my departure she had been cherishing the hope that I would never reappear, and had imagined all was fair sailing for her own to inherit name and wealth and position. I had surmised how she would feel, how she would fear a reconciliation should I succeed in seeing my father, and endeavor in every way to thwart me, hence my little stratagem which had succeeded so admirably.

I lost no time in opening the door and

entering my father's bedchamber. His couch was so situated that he could not see me, and he naturally concluded that it was my step-mother who had returned.

"What is the meaning of all this coil and clamor, Elisabetta?" said he, peevishly. "Have you been having another scene with Rinaldo? Of what new folly has he been guilty?"

"It is I, father," said I, now stepping to his bedside, "who was the cause of the noise. Signora della Verria did not wish me to see you."

He lifted himself upon his elbow and gazed at me, and I was shocked to note how emaciated he had become.

I did not know but that he would command me to leave him, but he said nothing, and after his eyes had traversed my figure from head to foot he sank back, drew a long breath, but still continued to look at me.

"I hope you will believe, sir," I said, "that I would not have forced myself into your presence had I not been going to make an important change in my life which it seemed right that you should know, and had I not had a story to relate to you to which I felt that you should listen.   But before speaking of these things I wish to tell you how deeply grieved I am to find you here."

"It is a place I shall never leave until I am carried to my grave.   I saw your grandfather lie thus for a half-year before he was borne on his last journey."

"And do the physicians give you no hope?"

"They can do nothing.   It is an affection of the blood.   Now I will hear what you have to say.   If my memory does not fail me, you promised not to set foot beneath this roof again until I recalled certain words I spoke at our last interview.   I have not recalled them — as yet."

All this, save the very last, was said in his old bitter and uncompromising way, and I found it hard to choke down the anger that rose in my breast, despite the fact that the sight of him lying there helpless awoke in me the sincerest pity.

Love for the man I could not feel. Never once, that I could recollect, had he done anything to inspire that emotion in my heart.

" I am about to quit service under the Visconti," I said, "to go to live at Padua with my mother's cousin, Alberto Gambacorta."

I expected an outburst at this, but none came.   All my father said was, —

" This cousin of yours was a fool when I knew him ! But I am glad you are quitting the Visconti."

" It is Signor Gambacorta's story I would tell you," I said.

" I think I know most of it," answered my father, " yet I will listen."

So I told him my cousin's story. There was silence in the room when I had done, and my father lay with closed eyes.

" She was a beautiful woman, your mother," he said at last, and now his look hung upon my face, " yet she never ceased to love him, her cousin, fool that he was. She loved him when she married me, thinking him dead, loved him and mourned for him during the early days of our life together. Do you wonder that a mad jealousy grew in my heart, for my love for her was an all-absorbing passion, a passion which even now in looking upon you I can recall in all its sweetness and bitterness! This jealousy wrecked what happiness might have been ours. It made me unreasonable and suspicious, it made her the more cold and retiring. I kept saying to myself, 'Toward another she may be all fire, toward me she is all ice.' I began to think, after a while, that perhaps it was not her cousin who had her love. 'She has seen some one else,' I told myself. At the time of the reappearance of Alberto Gambacorta, so deeply had the rust of jealousy eaten into my soul that I was ready to grasp at anything. Our encounter sobered me somewhat, but the demon still whispered at my ear; and all through my life at the thought of your mother, so all-demanding and so wholly barren of return was my love for her, the old flame has seared me.

Not until I had lain here for a month, and my flesh and my spirit been chastened, did I see with unobscured vision. The error was at the outset. I should never have married your mother; I, with my passionate disposition, should never have dreamed that I could be contented with the passive liking of a beautiful woman whose heart I knew had been another's, and was still his, though he was supposed to be dead. The marriage itself was the chief wrong. What followed was the natural and legitimate outcome."

My father paused, exhausted.

"Your mother, Luigi," said he, after a space, "was a blameless woman who deserved all the happiness the world could give, and yet who got little save sorrow and pain. What a strange world!

"You may wonder," he went on suddenly, "that realizing, as I must have done, my jealous disposition, I should marry again. It was partly to see if I could not forget, and Rinaldo's mother was one who had been devoted to me even before I met your mother in Padua. Of her affection I was sure."

"I hope I have your approval," I said, "in my decision to take up my abode in Padua."

"Yes; that is for the best. No doubt with the lapse of years your cousin is a changed man, and after what has passed you could not be happy here. But you shall have your rights, Luigi, after I am gone."

This last he said with a sudden vehemence.

"Only what was my mother's," I answered firmly. "In this decision nothing can move me. I shall not want, for I am to be my cousin's heir."

He looked earnestly at me for a little; then he said,—

"My end were more peaceful were it so, and yet—"

"It shall be so," I said. "I understand."

"You are too good to me, Luigi," he muttered.

Taking his dry and feverish hand

in mine, I rose from my seat at his bedside.

"Good by," said he.

I saw a look in his eyes I had never seen before, so I bent over and kissed him.

Chapter XV

The Black Closet

WHEN I reached my quarters in Milan, I found a messenger awaiting me, who summoned me to the palace at once. I was not surprised at this, thinking that my master had recovered from his indisposition, and either wished to hear a report of my mission to Padua, or desired to despatch me upon some further business. Hungry though I was, I set out on the messenger's heels, not dreaming that I should be long detained, picturing to myself what a fine dinner I should make a little later at the inn where I generally took my meals. Already the usual evening throng had begun to gather in the piazza, but to the gay scene I gave little heed. My thoughts flew forward to the interview which I expected to have that night with Signor Canaro, and to the glimpse I hoped to have of Angela.

At the head of the staircase I met Del Verme and the captain of the palace guard.

"His Lordship will see you directly, Della Verria," the former said.

"Has he quite recovered?" I asked.

"Not wholly. He bade me tell you to wait in the black closet. Put aside your sword and dagger. His Lordship is exceedingly nervous to-day, and does not like the sight of weapons."

I was surprised at neither of these commands, and yet there was something not quite natural in Del Verme's manner toward me, and I fancied that the captain of the guard looked at me askance.

The black closet was a small apartment to which my master not infrequently retired for meditation and study, and took its name from the fact that the hangings, the woodwork, and the furniture were all of black. The room was lighted by several small windows set high in the wall. Two doors gave access to it, one from the large reception-hall where Gian Galeazzo generally held his audiences, and the other from the last of the long suite of apartments which my master and his family occupied.

The reception-hall (it was the same room slightly changed in which Bernabo Visconti had received me) was empty, and though without the daylight was still fair, here the shadows had begun to gather, and a sensation of disquietude which was wholly unnatural stole over me. I was not wont to be thus visited by gloomy impressions, and was at a loss to account for the present uncomfortable feeling. With decided reluctance I parted with my sword and dagger, placing them upon a small table inlaid with jade which stood near the entrance to the black closet.

I had been in this room many times before, having frequently received my master's orders there, and was well aware that the doors worked by some peculiar mechanism. Neither door, so far as I knew, had a handle. One gained admission by the pressure of a spring, which caused a slipping back of bolts, whereupon the door swung inward. Of the actual working of the spring I was entirely ignorant. Formerly, when summoned to the black closet, I had tapped upon one of the panels, and presently been admitted. I now followed my usual custom, and a few seconds after I knocked, the door swung backward a little space, but quite sufficient to allow me to step inside. The place was empty, but had been occupied the instant before; for, as I entered, the door opposite closed so violently, that the gust of air from it caused the door behind me to shut with an ominous click.

Everything in the room seemed the same as when I had last visited it save that upon a stand in one corner there was a plentiful supply of fruit and bread, a large pasty, and a flagon of wine. As my eyes rested upon those eatables, like a flash the thought went through my brain, " I am a prisoner ! " There was good reason for Del Verme's asking me to put aside

my sword and dagger, and how unsus-
pectingly I had walked into the trap!

"Pish!" I said to myself, after a moment's consideration, "what folly! Why
should I be made a prisoner? Gian
Galeazzo is not ready to see me, and has
sent some one hither to admit me. He
will come himself after a little." And
yet I could not explain the presence of
the up-heaped table in the corner.

As time passed and no one appeared, I
grew uneasy. What Signor Canaro had
said, and furthermore what he had implied,
in regard to my master came to my mind
and would not be banished. Slowly the
light faded and darkness closed about me,
and still I heard no sound, so that gradually I was forced to the conclusion that
my first surmise had been correct. The
fruit and bread, the pasty and the wine,
had evidently been left there for me, so
I proceeded to attack them, and a very
good meal I made in spite of the disquieted state of my thoughts.

After I had carefully considered everything, I came to the conclusion that there

could be but one cause for my detention —and this was that my acquaintance with Signor Canaro and Angela was known to the Visconti, and he wished to keep me out of the way until he had worked his pleasure with them. Perhaps one of the bravos who had attacked Signor Canaro had recognized me; possibly the abode of father and daughter was watched, and I had been seen issuing from it. Then I fell to puzzling over the misfortunes of the Brescian. Assuredly, despite his wealth, his lot was far from being cast in pleasant places. Persecuted by Bernabo, now, for some unknown cause, he was being harried by his nephew and successor. But *was* the cause so difficult to understand? Gian Galeazzo was about entering upon what might prove an expensive campaign. There were new levies of troops to be raised, more mercenaries to be paid. True, the system of taxation which he had introduced yielded plentiful returns, but might he not have need of larger sums than he could put his hand upon? Who could say what plans,

what schemes for the future, were foment-
ing in that crafty brain?   Was it not the
riches of Signor Canaro that he was aim-
ing to obtain to enable him to carry out
his ambitious designs?

That he had some hold upon the Brescian I was certain, perhaps some claim
of doubtful validity which he proposed to
enforce.   At the thought of such baseness
and cowardice, such injustice, my heart
rose up within me.   "And this is the
man," I said to myself, "whom I have
been so delighted to serve!"

It had grown quite dark by this, and I
felt my way to a couch at one side of the
room, casting myself upon it in rage of
spirit.   Here I lay throughout the night,
catching bits of broken slumber, silently
storming at my impotence, wondering and
fearing what, in the interval, was happen-
ing to the two whose safety I had pledged
myself to guard.   Brave indeed must be
the man who can hold at bay the wolves
of doubt and fear through the long darkness from dusk to dawn if he be caged
and powerless to lift a hand.   Grisly tales

of the outrages practised by the tyrants of the day swarmed in upon my mind, and more than a score of times I fancied Signor Canaro murdered and Angela worse than dead. But hope leaped up in my heart with the first glimmer of the sun, only to sink again as the morning waned, and no one came to release me from my confinement Over every inch of the doors and casings did I go again and yet again in search for the hidden springs, and without avail. Though I knew it was useless, I beat upon the thick panels and cried out in my impatience and anger. I raged up and down my narrow quarters until well-nigh exhausted, finally to cast myself upon the couch, where I fell to biting my nails in silent despair.

So noon passed, and the afternoon wore away. Dejectedly I ate the last of the fruit and drained the flagon, and then began to wonder if my provisions would be replenished, or if I should still be held a prisoner and forced to fast, or if by any chance the hour of my release was at hand. I had now spent a night and a day in the black closet, and all my thoughts were by this time quite in harmony with the hangings and furnishings of the place. No sound from without had reached me so thick were the walls. Not even from the adjoining reception-hall did the slightest indication of noise come to my ears. It was as though I were in a place of the dead. Strange it would have been had my spirits been other than like a stream at its lowest ebb. A single sound, however, was enough to set them well toward flood,—a click which told of the moving of a spring. At last I should know if I had correctly surmised the cause of my detention. No longer should I be kept in suspense in regard to what to expect.

The door which swung back was that leading from the reception-hall, and the face I saw in the opening was that of Del Verme. He gave me an amused smile as he entered, and behind him I descried the Visconti, whose usually grave countenance was lit by a look I had not infrequently seen upon it, that of satisfaction over something achieved. I rose at their entrance, but gave them neither greeting nor salute.

"A little rest is good even for young limbs," said Del Verme, leaning upon the back of the deep chair into which my master sank. "His Lordship feared you might over-exert yourself, Della Verria, and so thought best to insure you a little quiet."

The soldier made no attempt to veil the irony of this speech, and my anger which had kindled at the sight of the two men flamed to a white heat at this.

"I should prefer choosing my own place of rest," I said, "and having ridden so far in his Lordship's service, I find myself indeed wearied, and do herewith tender to his Lordship my resignation from the position in his palace guard with which he deemed it fit some time since to honor me."

I saw by the faces of both the Visconti and Del Verme that my answer was un-expected. It was evident enough that they had no wish that I should give up my place as Gian Galeazzo's trusted mes-senger.

"You mistake Del Verme's meaning," said my master, in his most velvety tones. "I wish to be perfectly frank and fair with you, as I have always been. There was a little affair upon which you apparently inadvertently stumbled, a little lesson in the uselessness of persistent obstinacy which you may have misunderstood, but which was fully merited. It became necessary to carry out this little affair, to complete this little lesson; and to guard against your possible presence through a second inadvertence, or a further misunderstanding, it seemed best to ask you to remain here a few hours, a necessity which I most heartily regret. I tried to make you as comfortable as possible, and sincerely hope that the time did not hang heavily. Now that the matter of which I spoke is fully adjusted, I trust that you will be able to forget your tarry here, and that you will continue your duties as before. You know we are about adventuring upon a campaign in which there will be a rare chance for a young man like yourself to win both fame and fortune."

While my master was speaking, my temper cooled somewhat, and my mind worked rapidly. The chief part of my conclusions had been correct. I had been detained, so that without hinderance Gian Galeazzo could do what he willed with Signor Canaro, who, it appeared, had refused to comply with his demands. Now, more than ever, the Brescian and his daughter were in need of my aid. They were perhaps imprisoned somewhere. Was it not likely that I could be of more service to them if I made a pretence of still being on friendly terms with my master than as if I maintained the stand I had taken and insisted on resigning then and there? Perhaps he would have me watched for a while, but I would at least gain time, and would not be compelled to leave the city at once, as might be the case if I persisted in my decision to quit my position.

"I acknowledge that I was hasty in my determination," I said, "and I have no doubt that a few breaths of free air will suffice to blot all this incident from my memory."

I knew well enough when I spoke these words that nothing short of a complete lapsing of all recollection would cause me to forget what had occurred, and I pray that Christ and the Virgin have forgiven me the lie which never would have been uttered had I seen my way clear to avoid it.

"Ah, now the man of sense speaks!" cried the Visconti. "We shall see you a captain soon, shall we not, Del Verme?"

"Perhaps upon the day we take the field, if it is your Lordship's pleasure," answered the soldier.

"Thank you for the suggestion. I shall be as careful to remember as Della Verria is to forget."

I endeavored to express in fitting terms my appreciation of the new honor which they proposed to confer upon me, but much as I should have been elated at such a promotion a few months earlier, there was in it now no smack of sweetness. It would not do, however, to allow them to see this, and I flatter myself I carried off the deception well. As I ceased speaking, my master rose, and I knew the interview was at an end. He stepped toward the door, and it seemed to me that I heard the click of the spring before he had time to put hand upon panel or casing.

"It is not likely that I shall ever be trapped here again," I thought; "but if I am, the floor is the place where I shall look for that hidden spring."

"You will find your sword where you left it," said my master, standing aside for me to pass. "But stay!" he exclaimed, halting me in the doorway, and crossing the room he flung open a press which stood in a niche in one corner of the closet. Several cloaks hung therein, and one he lifted from the hook which held it."

"This," he said, handing it to me, "you might take with you."

It was my own cloak which had been caught up by the third of Signor Canaro's assailants in the Via San Lorenzo when the wretch had fled at the sound of nearing footsteps. In a flash it came to me who the man was. He was none other than the trooper whom Gian Galeazzo had bidden to prove my swordsmanship in the palace garden at Pavia, Otto von Ettergarde.

R

Chapter XVI

To the Rescue

AS I strode through the corridors of
the palace, I was amazed to think
that von Ettergarde had not entered my
mind before, now that I recalled certain
peculiarities of thrust and parry which had
struck me at our first meeting and again
at our encounter that night; and yet it
was several months since I had seen the
man, so mayhap it was not so strange that
I had not known him.   It was clear
enough now how my master had become
cognizant of my part in the affair of the
Via San Lorenzo.   Doubtless von Ettergarde had recognized the palace guardsman in my dress, and if he had not been
certain of my identity at first, my cloak,
which was of peculiar and marked style,

revealed my personality beyond a question.

A thrill of delight went through me as I felt the stones of the pavement beneath my feet, and saw the rose-tinted evening sky above my head. I sped toward my lodgings with all haste, feeling that I should probably be followed and my movements watched, yet confident that a little later, if I so desired, I could elude those who spied upon me.

I found the goodwife in whose house my quarters were situated standing at the street door.

"Here you are at last," said she. "There is a woman within who has been waiting to see you since early morning. She is in a sad state, poor thing, yet never a word will she tell me of her trouble."

"Quick!" cried I, "take me to her."

Along the passage the goodwife led me to her own apartments at the rear of the house. Here sat the woman of whom she had spoken, staring blankly out into a bare enclosure. As I had surmised, it was Angela Canaro's serving-maid. She turned as we entered, and, although the light was dim, recognized me at once. She sprang up with a cry of joy, and rushed toward me, falling upon her knees at my side and grasping one of my hands in both of hers.

"O Signore," she exclaimed, "you will save her, will you not, my sweet mistress? You will save her, will you not, Signore?"

Before I could win the story of what had happened from the woman's lips I had to promise that I would rescue Angela and her father — an assurance which was easy to give, but an undertaking which I was sure would be far from easy to accomplish.

It appeared from the woman's broken tale, which I finally succeeded in piecing together, that late the previous night a man had gained entrance to the abode of the Brescian and his daughter under the plea of being a messenger from the physician, who bore to the wounded man a lotion from his master. Once having gained admission to the house, he allowed six or eight masked men to enter, who speedily forced their way to the rooms of Signor Canaro, slaying the old serving-man, who offered resistance. Both father and daughter were seized and carried below, where horses were in waiting, which they were forced to mount. The woman had clung to her mistress and begged to be taken with her, but had been rudely thrown aside when the horsemen were ready to start. Just as they were about departing, Angela had leaned over and, in a whisper, bade her seek me out and tell me she thought they were to be taken to the Tower of Vezio. Where this was the woman did not know, nor could she say how her mistress had obtained her information.

Like the serving-maid, I was ignorant of the whereabouts of the tower, but that was a small matter. Hartzheim would doubtless know, or be able to find out readily, and on him I counted for assistance. How far he would be willing to aid me I could not say, but I determined at once to set out in search of him, and relate to him the whole story. Certainly the knowledge of the destination of the kidnappers was a great point gained, and I blessed my forethought in telling Angela where my lodgings were, else had I not come by this so speedily. She had probably overheard one of her captors let fall the name of the tower, and had grasped it as being the place where she and her father were likely to be imprisoned. I concluded from the serving-woman's account of the treatment they received, that they were in no immediate danger of their lives, unless the fatigue of horseback riding should affect Signor Canaro unfavorably, and ascended to my rooms considerably heartened at what I had heard.

I put aside my guardsman's dress, donned a shirt of linked mail, then selected a doublet of dark stuff with trunks and hose to match. My garb being to my satisfaction, I secured what gold I possessed, together with my few trinkets, about my person, and was ready to set out. Below stairs I paused for a last word with the woman. Calling the good-wife of the house aside, I put several pieces of gold into her hand and bade her care for the unfortunate serving-maid until she should be sent for. Should no one come for her after a space of two months, I begged the goodwife to interest herself in obtaining her a position. To the serving-woman herself I renewed my assurance that I would find her mistress, and that when I had seen her in a place of safety she should be allowed to join her again.

Except the man at the stable who had charge of Hawkwood I employed no servant, — though I had intended to when I changed my quarters, — and I now had reason to be thankful that I was totally unhampered. Instead of seeking egress to the street by the common entrance, I passed from the rear of the house into the small enclosure behind it, and thence to the back room of a small wine-shop, which had a door opening upon a crooked ally. Picking my way along this dim passage, I finally emerged in a thoroughfare well lighted and gayly peopled. Slipping on the mask which I had found in the piazza and taken care to preserve, I hurried off toward Hartzheim's quarters. If a watch had been set upon me I was sure that I had eluded scrutiny. I had not been able to see Hartzheim since my return from Padua, and was by no means sure where to look for him. Though I knew he was rarely at his lodgings, I thought perhaps his man might be able to give me some clew to his whereabouts. Hence it was thither I first turned my steps.

As I ascended the stairs which led to the rooms of my friend, there came down to me a gay burst of laughter, and then the loud chorus of a drinking-song. I halted in vexation of spirit. Hartzheim was giving a supper to some of his German comrades. For my purpose nothing could have been more inopportune. What should I do? Hartzheim I must see, and without delay, for in him lay my only hope of assistance. But to show myself to his companions, with some of whom I no doubt had at least a slight acquaintance, was far from my desire. However, no other course seemed open ; so, deciding to trust the outcome to fortune and determining, unless absolutely forced to do so, not to remove my mask, I mounted to the top of the stairs and struck a bold summons on the door. Above the din I heard the host's cry of "Enter!" So I swung back the heavy oak, and advanced a pace within the doorway.

Through the reek of candle fumes and the flare of the flames, I made out the faces of five troopers gathered with my friend about a table on which, in the centre of the fragments of a feast, stood a huge flagon of the red Tuscan chianti. The effect caused by my appearance was like that of a ghost at a banquet, which perhaps was little to be wondered at, for, coming in upon them suddenly in my sombre garb and black mask, I undoubtedly seemed for a moment like an uncanny visitant from a dark world concerning which men are wont to speak with bated breath.

Two of the troopers sprang up with exclamations of fright, a third started back in his chair and nearly upset the table, while Hartzheim, less superstitious than the rest, angry at being interrupted, and not dreaming who I was, roared out an oath, and demanded what I wanted.

"My business," said I, "is with the Signor Hartzheim."

Still he did not know me, for he rose from his seat and came toward the door in no very good-humored fashion.

"Well," he exclaimed, "be short! You see I am engaged."

"It is a matter of great importance," said I, boldly, "and for your ear alone."

"Ah!" he cried, his whole air changing as he now recognized my voice. "Come this way. My friends will pardon us if we withdraw for a moment."

He led me into his sleeping-room and closed the door.

"What, in the name of the saints, is the meaning of all this mystery?" said he, as I removed my mask.

"That I am in great trouble, and want, your advice," I answered, thinking it best to put it in that way.

"What has happened?"

"It will take me some time to explain. Where can I see you, and how soon?"

He thought a moment.

"Stay where you are," he said. "I will send these fellows packing. Some of them have already had more wine than is good for them. I will tell them you bring an important message from Gian Galeazzo which compels me to ask them to postpone the rest of our festivities. That will satisfy them."

He left me hurriedly, and presently I heard the troopers descending the stairs, none too steadily some of them. Then the door was flung open.

"Now you may come out," my friend exclaimed.

We seated ourselves, and he poured me a cup of wine.

"Take that," said he. "You look as though you needed it to pull yourself together."

I swallowed a part of the draught he offered me, and then began my story. As I proceeded, he rose, and paced the room, questioning me occasionally.

"It is a dastardly deed!" he cried, when I had finished. "I suppose you think of trying to rescue the girl and her father?"

"Yes," I answered; "I am willing to risk life — all — for her an hundred times over."

"The rescue will not be an easy matter, but it will be vastly easier if they are confined in the Tower of Vezio than it would be if they were secreted here."

"You know where the tower is, then?"

"Yes, I have seen it. It overlooks the lake of Como just above where the two arms of the lake join. In time gone by it has sometimes been garrisoned by the rulers of Milan to enforce their over-lordship of that region, but I am sure there is no garrison in it now."

"Advise me, Hartzheim," I cried: "you are full of resources. Tell me what I had best do."

He was silent for a space, then he came and offered me his hand.

"I will do more than that," he said; "I will help you."

I leaped to my feet with an exclamation of joy.

"I had hoped you would," I cried, "but I would not breathe the hope. I felt I should be asking you to sacrifice too much."

"I confess," said he, "that I have had great expectations from this war in which the Visconti is about to engage. If I aid you I put behind me all rewards that might come from a successful campaign, but pouf! there will be other wars, and there are other masters quite as willing to pay for a good sword and a stout arm."

"But you are not considering what might happen in case we should fail," said I, "and you should fall into Gian Galeazzo's hands."

"Fail!" he cried. "I' faith, you are a pretty lover to talk of failing when you are about to set out to rescue your mistress."

"I was thinking of the consequences to you, and not of myself," said I.

He picked up his beaker of wine.

"A toast!" he cried. "Here's health to *La bella Signorina*, and confusion to the Great Viper!

"Now to business," he continued, as we put down our empty cups. "We should be on the road north by midnight, or soon after, and in the meanwhile there is much to be looked to. It is advisable that you keep out of sight, so you had better let me make the necessary arrangements. There is a little inn called the Triton, near the Vercellina gate, which I presume you know. I will secure horses and have them sent thither, and will meet you there at eleven, or thereabouts. Do you hasten thither at once and keep under cover until I come. We shall need a bite before we start, for a night's ride on an empty stomach is an ill medicine for the digestion, so bid the landlord have a stuffed fowl or a rabbit ready, against my arrival, in one of his rooms above stairs."

I was not slow to do my friend's bidding, and presently I was sitting in a cosy little apartment in the Triton (the very inn where I had paused for a draught of wine on the morning of my mission to Milan), waiting with impatience well in curb, for the appearance of Hartzheim.

The moonlight spattered with silver the open space in front of the inn, and the water made a pleasant gurgle in the stone drinking-basin. Unseen by the comers and goers, I watched the tide of patronage slacken as the hour grew late, my thoughts leaping forward along the northward track we were to follow. I gritted my teeth as I dwelt upon Angela Canaro in the hands of Gian Galeazzo's band of kidnappers, exposed to I knew not what insults and indignities, and longed for the time to come when we should be in the saddle with the south wind at our backs. I could but admire Hartzheim's foresight in choosing the Vercellina gate for our exit from the city. We should both be missed before the morning was many hours old, and an immediate inquiry be instituted. If it were discovered, as it doubtless would be, that horsemen had ridden forth at midnight from the gateway leading toward

Pavia, suspicion in regard to our real destination might be averted. Yet I had a notion that as soon as the Visconti learned of my disappearance he would despatch an admonition of caution to the one commanding the men at the tower, in which case it behooved us to hasten. We should have scant time to elaborate a plan of rescue. A bold, quick stroke would have to be depended upon.

Before the last guest left the wine-room, a man leading three horses turned into the open space before the inn. In the man I made out Hartzheim's servant, Galbo, who was evidently to accompany us, and among the horses much to my delight I discovered Hawkwood, seemingly no longer lame. I hoped my friend was not far behind, but it was fully an hour, and hard upon midnight, before I beheld his stalwart bulk in the doorway of the apartment.

" I was delayed," said Hartzheim, " for I had to assure a little woman I would send for her when I was safely settled in Padua or Venice," and the great fellow smiled rather sheepishly.

" Ah," said I, to whom this was wholly in the nature of a surprise, "so Mars is ruled by Venus, after all ! "

" Well, you see," he explained, " I had promised her that after this campaign we would have a cosy place somewhere to ourselves, a tidy little inn like this, maybe."

Then I saw what a sacrifice he was making in my behalf, and broke out, telling him that I would not allow it ; but he silenced me in his careless, kindly way, saying now, knowing what he did, he would not serve Gian Galeazzo if his Lordship offered him the command of all his forces.

After this we fell to discussing the stuffed fowl which the landlord had brought in steaming, and presently Galbo appeared to say that the horses were ready. Hartzheim bade his man finish the fowl, then we hurried below, and having settled our reckoning, went forth to mount. Hawkwood poked his velvety nose up to my face as I adjusted his bridle, and I called him what he was, and still is, the prince of horses.

There was but a brief halt at the gate, for Hartzheim told the keeper in so authoritative a way that we rode upon his Lordship's business that he did not venture to question us. Soon we were cutting a wide arc about the city walls, and erelong the hoofs of our horses were beating in rhythmic unison upon the Como road.

Chapter XVII

The Encounter at Como

DAWN was breaking when we rode into Como and halted at the Sign of the Carp upon the lake quay. I was moved by the beauty of the scene, the like of which I had never before looked upon. There was a flush of mingled rose and gold upon the water, and the sails of the outgoing fisher boats were like great delicately tinted wings in the wondrous light. There was no one astir about the inn, but we were not long in rousing a hostler who took charge of our horses, and as we turned from the stable the landlord appeared, rubbing the sleep from his eyes.

"A fair day to you, gentlemen," said he. "Such early travellers deserve all the good things fortune provides.   It is a sorry thing to have to ride by night."

"It is sorry indeed," said I, "unless there be a hot flitch waiting at the end of the journey."

"Such may be found here, and of the best, by any that have the coin to pay for it."

"Then rouse your cook, and bid him stir his fire," we cried, and while the landlord set out to do our bidding we strolled down to the water's edge, having in mind to look for a boat that would suit our purpose.   We were still examining the shipping when he hailed us with the announcement that our meal was ready.   As we passed into the room where it was being served, we heard a stir in the apartment above, and Hartzheim remarked to the landlord that some of his guests were moving early.

"Yes," that worthy said, "they are two troopers who remained behind to purchase provisions; their comrades, who were escorting a lady and gentleman, some invalid lord and his lady on their way to their castle, went up the lake yester noon."

I forbore to look at Hartzheim when I heard this, for fear that I should show some exultation at the news. There was now no doubt but that we were on the right track.

My friend made no immediate response to the landlord's words, but halted in the middle of the room as though he were listening to what was going on overhead. The men were evidently dressing. Suddenly he turned.

"This is our chance," he said in a whisper to me; then to the landlord, "I have some business with the gentlemen above. I am quite sure they are the ones. Will you kindly show me to their door. Our breakfast can wait."

Not only was our host surprised, but he seemed little inclined to fall in with Hartzheim's wishes. I saw his eyes move furtively, as though he either thought of making a dash from the room, or of calling some one to his assistance. But Hartzheim's manner changed, as it could on occasion, from the blandly agreeable to the bristling and ferocious.

"You heard me," he roared; "by heaven, be quick, or you go for a morning bath off the quay yonder!"

The man's knees began to shake.

"Certainly, certainly," he stammered; "I did not quite understand, you were so sudden."

"You had best watch the window, Luigi," said my friend, as he followed our now obliging host.

From my post without I heard them ascend the stairs, and then came Hartzheim's knock upon the door, which was followed by a parley of some length. Presently the shutters above were unfastened, and a pair of eyes looked down at me, but were hurriedly withdrawn. After a silence of considerable duration I heard Hartzheim's summons anew, this time more emphatic than before, and I judged that instead of his knuckles he was using his sword hilt. Directly there was the clatter of hurriedly descending feet. I rushed within just in time to arrest the steps of the landlord, who was bolting toward the rear entrance of the inn, evidently bent upon going in search of some of the town authorities. I let him see the edge of my bare blade, and he began to whimper like a whipped cur.

"Listen!" cried I, still gripping him by the collar. "Not a glimpse of an augustal will you get for that fine breakfast that is cooling if you try to thwart us further; but if you are quiet, we will see that you have triple pay."

"But the reputation of my house!"

"Rubbish!" said I; "there is no one abroad at this hour, and we mean no harm to the troopers above. We merely wish to assure ourselves that they will not harm us."

The promise of so abundant a recompense for his cookery quite won him over; but I had done with my little interview none too soon, for as I released him there rang out a shout for aid from Hartzheim. With my drawn weapon in hand I sprang into the hallway. As I did so there came the fierce clash of steel from above, and up the stairs I flew in hot-footed haste. I made out three forms, in the dim light, in one corner of the broad landing, my friend with his back to the wall calmly beating off the vicious attack of two men.

"Turn!" cried I, pricking one of them upon the buttock, whereat he wheeled about with a snort of rage, and charged upon me like a bull.

"Disarm your man," called Hartzheim to me, and I engaged my antagonist with that intent. While he who faced me was a good swordsman as troopers go, he knew none of the fine arts of fence in which I had taken so much pains to perfect myself. I thought I should be able to effect my end without letting him feel my point, but he had a tenacious grip, and, moreover, knew what I was trying to do. I heard the weapon of Hartzheim's adversary fall with a ring-ing vibration upon the floor, and, deter-mining not to keep my friend long waiting, I practised a little feint which a skilful Frenchman had taught me, ripped up my opponent's sword-arm, and had him wholly at my mercy.

"We will go in here," said Hartzheim, pointing to the open door of the room which the two men had occupied.

At my friend's bidding the two disarmed troopers passed into the apartment, and we followed them, having first secured their swords and forced them to surrender their daggers. From their faces I saw that they were Germans, and from their garb that they belonged to the company in which von Ettergarde was an officer.

"We regret putting you to any inconvenience, comrades," said Hartzheim, "but we shall have to ask you to change clothes with us, and then we shall wish you to answer a few questions. You will of course see the folly of refusing."

The men made no reply.

"Come," said my friend, "bestir yourselves. We have no time to spare."

Sullenly the troopers began to divest themselves of their apparel, and soon the change was effected, we having, during the process, bound up the arm of the one whom I had wounded, his hurt proving to be quite an ugly cut. Hartzheim's new garb suited him well, but mine was not just to my liking, the hose being somewhat too ample. However, I knew that the change was part of a plan my friend had in mind, and it did not enter my head to demur.

"Now," said Hartzheim, after the readjustment in dress had been completed, "suppose you tell us under whose orders you are acting."

"Von Ettergarde's," said one, without hesitation.

"And how many men are there at the tower?"

"Eight, counting the keeper and his assistant."

"You were to go on to-day with provisions, I understand. Where is your boat?"

"Yonder at the quay."

"And the provisions?"

"Were to be put on board this morning."

"At what hour were you to start?"

"By noon, if the wind favored."

"Good! we will give you the pleasure of our company."

The troopers made such wry faces at this information that both Hartzheim and I shouted with laughter.

"I fear you do not appreciate the honor we are doing you," my friend said, — a bit of pleasantry which was quite lost upon them.

Hartzheim remained to guard our prisoners while I went below and breakfasted, returning to allow him to satisfy his hunger. Then, when the troopers had been fed, we fastened their feet and hands securely, and set Galbo to watch over them while we caught a few hours of sleep, bidding my friend's man call us if his charges attempted to move or make an outcry. Our liberality had quite won over the landlord, who was now eager to meet our lightest wish, so we stretched ourselves out with the feeling that all was going well.

I dropped straightway into a dream in which, single-handed, I rescued Angela

Canaro from a dozen men-at-arms, and bore her, strange to say, not to my home in Padua, but to my father's house in Pavia, where my father appeared at the door and kissed her hand, leading her up the staircase to the grand hall; there, as I looked about for the lowering countenance of my step-mother, a beautiful lady came forward and took my beloved in her arms, saying, "I am Luigi's mother, and will love you because you love him."

It was not far from the stroke of noon when Galbo came to awaken us; and both of us rose, alert for action. Repairing to the quay, we found the boat which the troopers had pointed out to us, prepared to start on a moment's notice.

"Who hired you, my men?" said Hartzheim to the four sailors who were lounging upon the thwarts.

"A Signore who went up the lake yesterday," answered one of them.

"And he paid you?"

"No; he is to pay us when we deliver the cargo."

"Well, if you will do as the Signore

here and I wish you to, and ask no questions, we will double the sum offered you, and perhaps give you further employment after this present voyage is over."

The four men looked at one another an instant. For further consultation there seemed to be no need.

"Agreed! Signore," they cried in a chorus.

"Very good," said Hartzheim. "Remember you are to obey us, and there are to be no questions asked."

"We will remember. And the money?"

"That will be forthcoming, you need have no fear. Here is earnest of full payment," and Hartzheim dropped a gold piece into the spokesman's palm.

When we returned to the inn, we found Galbo had saddled the horses and was prepared to start. We had decided that it would be best to send him with the horses across the country to Lecco to await our coming there at an inn of which Hartzheim knew. Furthermore, my friend had given his man orders to procure two additional steeds; for, if our quest were successful, our party would number five when we set out from Lecco for Padua, which was to be our destination. Although the Lord of Padua had entered into an alliance with the Visconti, I knew well that there was nothing to be feared from the latter when once we were within the walls of the city ruled by Francesco da Carrara.

Having seen Galbo depart, we haled forth our prisoners. Fastening them together arm to arm, and threatening them with a taste of bare steel if they attempted to escape, or made any outcry, we marched them before us to the quay and saw them safely bestowed in a clear space in the bow of the boat. There was a group of curious on-lookers, but no one ventured to interfere. Such spectacles were not uncommon, and our garb gave us authority in the public mind. One of the town watch approached, and to satisfy his unspoken curiosity Hartzheim told him we were under orders from his Lordship, the Visconti, whereat with a few commonplace remarks he continued on his way. I did not know but that the troopers might appeal to him for aid, but with so wholesome a dread had my friend inspired them that they did not open their lips. Evidently they thought it best to bide their time, meditating perhaps a break for freedom when we had reached the end of the voyage and they were near their comrades. Had they surmised our intentions in regard to them, possibly we should have encountered something other than tame submission.

The boatmen now adjusted the long oars with which our little craft was fitted, and pulled a short distance out into the bay, where the broad sail was run up. A gust filled this, the water began to ripple with a pleasant murmur against the prow, the city receded, and soon, rounding a headland, the full beauty of this wonderful lake broke upon me, the grand mountains, the luxuriantly wooded shores, and the liquid expanse in which both were mirrored and over which we glided as though sailing some paradisial lake of dream.

Chapter XVIII

Up the Lake

I HAD one great consolation as I sat in the shadow of the sail and watched the lovely panorama of the shores unfold and slip by. I drew my solace from the words of the innkeeper at Como, who had spoken of Angela and her father as a lord and his lady going to their castle. It was evident, from the way he regarded them, that they had been treated with consideration on their journey from Milan. This led me to hope that they would meet with no ill usage before we could effect their rescue. I was considerably puzzled over what might be the Visconti's ultimate intention in regard to his prisoners, whether he proposed to detain them only until he could bend Vincenzo Canaro to his will, or whether it was his purpose to keep them confined either for a brief or for a considerable period, and then let it appear that they had died a natural death when in reality some subtly administered poison was responsible for their taking off. I concluded, after long meditation, that they were in no immediate danger, and that von Ettergarde's murderous assault on Signor Canaro in the Via San Lorenzo had not been a part of the original plan, but was suddenly inspired by the fact that he saw the man whom he had been ordered to seize was likely to escape from his clutches.

The breeze continued fair, and our progress was such that Hartzheim and I agreed we were likely to reach our destination long before it was desirable; so beyond Nesso, yet before we reached the promontory of La Cavagnola, we put into a little bay where a mountain stream emptied, coming down from the heights of Monte Colmenacco. Above us the chestnut groves were feathery with fragrant flowers, while about us were laurel copses in which the birds ever and anon broke out in a silvery intermezzo.

How restful it was, after the stress of the night and morning, to relax our tense nerves for a little in that placid seclusion, and watch the sun slowly dip toward the crest of the mountain-chain! After a little a roseate light was shed over the water, and, bathed in the flood of the afterglow, we began to make preparation for getting under way again.

"Comrades," said Hartzheim to the two troopers, who had preserved a moody silence during the whole of our tarry, " I regret that we must part company, but such is the present necessity. You will kindly step on shore. If you object to the grass for a bed and the laurel boughs for a roof, there is Nesso a few miles back, where doubtless there are lodgings a-plenty."

So surprised were our prisoners that for a moment they sat gazing at my friend incredulously, scarce believing their ears. The two sailors upon the beach, who had braced themselves to push off the boat, relaxed their bodies and stepped back so that the troopers might land. A dumb rage kindled in the eyes of these men. They looked from one to the other of us and found us smiling; the boatmen, too, were grinning amusedly. They were unarmed, and knew that they must obey, but when they were once on shore, beyond our reach, and the boat was again floated, they flung curses long and loud at us across the water, vowing vengeance if they had to follow us to the ends of the earth.

"Their tempers will be somewhat cooled by morning," said Hartzheim, "and in any event I trust by that time we shall be far away."

The wind died with the going down of the sun, so the sail was hauled in and the long oars adjusted. There was a music to me in their rise and dip, they were lifted so evenly and fell in such perfect unison; and I heard Hartzheim, moved, too, by the sense of harmony above and about us, humming to himself some song of his northland home. Thus for a brief space we were removed, even as we had been that afternoon in the little bay girt by the shining laurels, from the bitter rancors of the world.

By and by we passed the promontory that juts into the lake where the Como and Lecco arms join, and not long afterward one of the boatmen pointed out to us some lights that twinkled through the dusk a short distance ahead, upon the right.

"That is the landing-place, Signori," said he, "and there," lifting his finger to other lights far up the impending slope, "is the village of Vezio and the tower."

Our destination was at hand. As I raised my eyes to the gleaming points beaconing through the night from the mountain side, my heart went out up the path of the rays to the prison of my beloved, and I longed to be ashore striking a bold blow for her release.

The situation demanded immediate action. Delay would be fatal to our hopes. The men whom we had left behind near Nesso would find means of continuing their journey on the morrow, and indeed by that time word of warning might come to von Ettergarde from Milan. But now by some piece of good fortune we might take the captors of Signor Canaro and his daughter unaware, and either by a ruse, or by a sudden and unexpected stroke, effect our end. To plan, however, was impossible until we had at least in a measure reconnoitred.

As we turned into the small harbor formed by a stream called the Esino, which here debouches, we noted two men close to the water's edge who seemed to be watching us intently. Presently one of them hailed us.

" Are you from Como ? " he called.

" Yes, Signore," answered one of the boatmen.

" Is it you, Mandell and Pfänder ? " cried the speaker.

" No," said Hartzheim, with ready tongue ; " Mandell and Pfänder returned to Milan. We have come on in their stead with orders from his Lordship to the officer in command here."

We could see that they were surprised at this, for we had now drawn quite near the stone wall of the place of landing. They conferred a moment, then one of them said, —

"Who are you? We don't recognize your voice."

"Hartzheim," answered my friend; "and Stainer is with me," he added, giving me the name of one of the men in his own command.

Who Hartzheim was they knew well, and they were apparently satisfied, for they waited for the boat to draw up alongside the rude quay.

"We must seize these fellows," said my companion, in a low tone, "or they may make trouble for us. With them out of the way there will be two less to deal with at the tower."

The prow of the boat touched the wall, and with a rope in hand one of the sailors sprang to land, casting the line which he held around a post firmly set in the earth. The other sailors were busy unshipping their oars, and when two of them went toward the bow Hartzheim called to the men above, —

"Come down and lend us a hand with these stores. We had best put them ashore ourselves."

They complied without hesitation or demur. It was several feet from the quay to the boat, and before the unsuspecting troopers had recovered from the necessary spring my friend and I had leaped upon them. Hartzheim bore his man down without difficulty, choking him into speedy submission, but I was hardly so fortunate. My strength was far from being equal to that of my comrade, and it proved that my antagonist was the stouter of the two troopers. To and fro we struggled, each endeavoring to throw the other to the bottom of the boat. I had the advantage in the hold, else had it speedily gone ill with me; yet in spite of this, strive as I would, I could not force my adversary down. I felt him fumbling for his dagger, and failing in that he tried to tear me from him and fling me into the lake. But I clung to him like a leech, and finally, getting the wall as a prop for my back, I locked one leg behind him, threw my whole weight against him, and over we went together, his head in the descent striking upon one of the thwarts with tremendous force. His hold upon me relaxed, and he sank into a limp heap, unconscious.

All this struggle went on without an outcry, and was witnessed only by the four boatmen, who offered neither to assist nor to restrain us. When our captives had been secured and gagged, and placed in the bow, where their bodies were well-nigh hidden by a piece of sail-cloth, we handed the sailors their promised wage. Now, however, when we proposed to hire them further, they demurred, and we saw that they were inclined to be frightened at what they had done, feeling perhaps that they might be implicated in our somewhat high-handed proceedings.

" These men, Signori, and those others, are they not in the employ of his Lordship of Milan?" asked one of them. " We know not what you aim to do, but truly it will go hard with us if his Lordship discovers it was our boat that brought you hither."

I saw what might be the sole chance of escape, were the rescue safely effected, slipping away from us.

"Your fears are but idle!" I cried. "We, too, are in his Lordship's employ, and are striving to set free a Signore and his daughter who have been wrongfully confined up yonder in the tower. If you will agree to take us to Lecco to-night, your pockets shall be so heavy with gold that not one of you will need to work again for a year."

I realized that plain speaking alone would win them wholly to our side, and my open statement of the case had the desired effect; for after a short conference their spokesman announced that they would run the risk and place their boat at our disposal. Accordingly, having bidden them lighten the craft of most of the provisions and await us where they were, we hastened to mount the quay.

"We must find a guide," said my friend.

"I would that we might chance upon some sturdy fellow who would lend us the aid of his stout arm on a pinch."

Even as Hartzheim spoke, we heard a voice trolling out a rollicking stave, —

"O a trooper's life, O a trooper's life,
     Is the life that's fair and free!
   In the prick o' the press, in the stress o' the
         strife,
   With his own true blade by his side for a
         wife, —
   O a trooper's life for me!"

Then out of the shadow there strode a burly form.

"Ho, comrade!" called Hartzheim, "though I know you not, I'll wager a florin that you have couched a lance or trailed a pike at the wars! Come, drink with us a cup to the peace of the soul of the last knave you spitted."

"That I would gladly, friends," said the man, approaching us, "were I not just recovered from a wound, and hence forced to be most abstemious lest the pestilent fever take hold on me again."

"I was quite right about the wars, then!" said Hartzheim.

"You were, in truth," said the man, who proved to be a seemly looking fellow, perhaps ten years my senior. There was a smack of importance in his manner, but his air of bravado was not offensive and was explained later when we discovered that this was his home and birthplace. "A dozen years," he exclaimed, "have I worn a morion!"

"Under what lord or lords, if the question give no offence?"

"None, i' faith. Can Signorio and Antonio della Scala have been my masters. You serve the Visconti, by your dress. Erelong we may be at one another's throats, if the jade, Rumor, has it right; for already when I left Verona, three weeks since, it was said that Gian Galeazzo had joined Francesco da Carrara against the Lord of Verona."

"Rumor in this case speaks truly, but there is small likelihood that the clash of arms will find us under the banner of the Visconti. My friend here has little cause to love him, and I am wholly of his mind."

"Ah, haply then you will join me! I go back to Verona in a few days. This is my old home, and I am here recruiting from a wound a cursed Paduan pikeman gave me. I can assure you of a warm welcome by the Adige, my master being eager to add to his following."

"It is most gracious of you to suggest it, but we have that on hand which will, I fear, prevent us from joining you."

I began now to see toward what Hartzheim was leading.

"Some private affair, no doubt," said the follower of Antonio della Scala.

"Yes," answered my friend; "it is of that nature, and I do not mind telling you that if you would strike a blow at your master's enemy, the Visconti, you could not do so more easily than by aiding us for an hour."

"For an hour!"

"If we succeed, we shall not be longer than that. Our little affair calls us up yonder to the tower."

"Ah, a lord and lady arrived yesterday! I saw them land. They are prisoners, perhaps?"

"Exactly! and we propose to rescue them; but we need a guide, a decoy, one who would be willing to make some sort of an outcry, and attract the attention of those guarding them."

"You may command me!" cried the man. "I am wholly at your service. My sword has been rusting for days, and my muscles are beginning to ache from sloth. As for the wound, it must stand the test some time, and why not now?"

"But we look to do the fighting!" I exclaimed. "We could not think of asking a man just recovering from a wound to endanger himself."

"My friend is quite right," said Hartzheim. "If you will act as guide and decoy, we will manage to take care of the rest."

"Well," said our obliging ally, whose name we discovered to be Leo Berni, "I flatter myself that I can strike a very pretty blow, and if you find that you need my sword, I beg that you will not hesitate to call on me."

We thanked him most heartily for the chivalrous spirit which he manifested, and without delay, following closely in his footsteps, struck into a sharply ascending path, which at first wound along the right bank of the Val d' Esino, but finally mounted and traversed the crest of the ridge.

Chapter **XIX**

The Tower of Vezio

THE darkness was intense, for the night had become cloudy, and had our guide not been perfectly familiar with the pathway, it would have been a miracle had we reached Vezio in safety. There were barriers to be avoided, and we passed more than one spot where a mis-step meant a broken arm or leg, if not a broken neck. After what seemed an interminable and arduous scramble, the barking of a dog told us that we were not far from the village which stood near the tower. Presently the path widened, and we distinguished the dark outline of houses with lights burning in a few of the upper windows. The gloom below, how-ever, was scarcely perceptibly broken, and we still had to grope our way painfully.

"I thought it might be well to avoid the main street," said our guide, "so I have chosen this route, which is the shortest, though far from pleasant. You had best keep close to me."

As we passed between the houses, the dank air of open cellars cast a chill upon us, while the reeking breath of the gutters seemed likely to choke us with its foulness. We stumbled over heaps of garbage, twice blundered against tipsy foot-farers, who cursed us thickly, and at length won an open space from which we could clearly distinguish the massive bulk and crenelated battlements of the tower. In front of it there seemed to be a sort of platform upon which a fire had evidently been kindled, for a fitful light radiated from the spot which caused the walls to stand out against the inky background of the night.

"The ordinary approach to the tower is upon the right, but this will best serve your present purpose," said Berni, leading us into a dip where grew some gnarled trunks which we made out to be olive trees.

Soon we were at the base of a sort of terrace, and could hear the murmur of voices. Bidding us wait where we were for a brief space, our guide slipped away into the darkness. Between Hartzheim and myself no word was spoken. With his head craned to one side my friend listened intently for a sign of Berni's return, while I kept my eyes fixed upon the small dark windows of the tower, which now loomed above us, wondering if from any of them Angela Canaro were at that moment looking down. Inspired by the cheer of Hartzheim's presence, and by the singularly good fortune which had attended our enterprise from the very outset, up to this time I had allowed no doubt in regard to our ultimate success to enter my mind; but now as I gazed at the gloomy massiveness of my beloved's prison, and realized that, unless favored by chance, six stout men must be overcome before she could be set free, a sudden fear seemed to clutch my heart, and I thought, "What if we should fail?"

By daylight, amid familiar or plainly discernible surroundings, most men (those, that is, who are worthy to be classed with the stronger sex) can meet peril unmoved, or feel a sense of exhilaration in the face of danger; but begirt by darkness and environed by uncertainty, I have heard old soldiers say that their wonted calmness and valor forsook them. It is with this knowledge that I console myself when I recall my faint-heartedness as I stood in the murk beneath the Tower of Vezio and awaited the return of Leo Berni.

My mind, packed with sombre forebodings, was beginning to entertain suspicions of his trustworthiness, when he emerged before us out of the darkness.

"If you will come with me," he said, "and step softly, you may be able to hear something that will interest you. After you have listened you can form your plans."

Hanging hard upon his footsteps, we skirted the base of the terrace, and presently, having rounded a projection, the reflection cast by the fire upon the platform showed us, a score of paces distant, the path of approach from the village. Above, and close at hand, we heard voices.

"I will wait here," said our guide. "If you are careful, you can get within earshot without being detected."

The slope of the terrace was partially set with a low growth of laurels, beneath which the earth was soft. Dropping upon our hands and knees, Hartzheim and I worked our way slowly upward. So cautious were we that I doubt if we made a sound, and if we did, it must have been lost in the crackling of the flames; for when we reached the summit of the terrace and could peer over, the two men who sat upon the bench a dozen feet away were still intent on their conversation. One of them I made out to be von Ettergarde. For a moment I could not catch what they were saying, their backs being turned toward us, so I let my eyes rove about the open space in the centre of which the fire was burning. Why this had been kindled was now evident, a host of spinning midges being visible in the air high above the flames. The entrance to the tower was situated in that corner of the building nearest the village of Vezio. Through the open doorway I could detect a shifting glimmer which told me that the room was torch-lit. Two men were seated on the entrance threshold, while two others were lounging on the steps below. Those in the doorway wore a different garb from the others, who were dressed like ourselves, so I concluded that one must be the keeper of the tower and the other his assistant.

My roving glance was arrested by von Ettergarde's words.

"It is agreed upon, then," I heard him say. "You will look after the girl while I am gone to Milan to claim the reward for the little affair."

"Yes," answered the other, "provided half the money is mine."

"You fool," cried von Ettergarde, angrily, "how many times must I tell you that the division shall be equal!"

"It is a goodly sum, and worth the

risk ; but if the Visconti should discover the deceit, and we should be taken, it makes my blood creep to think of what he would do to us."

An exclamation of impatience fell from von Ettergarde's lips.

" You faint-hearted dolt," he cried, " can you not see that discovery is impossible ? By Bacchus, I would that I had spoken to one of the others and not to you ! "

" If you will confide the plan more fully, I shall feel greater confidence."

So evident was it that some villany not meditated even by the Lord of Milan was on foot that I wriggled a trifle nearer, lest any word should escape my ears.

" It is to be done to-morrow night, as I told you," von Ettergarde said, in a most matter of fact tone, " unless orders to the contrary come from Milan. But instead of making way with the girl after the sleeping potion has been administered, she shall not be harmed. I shall see that an extra dose of the drug is given her so she will not waken until she is safe in the vault of the tower. As you and I are to have the affair in hand, no one can discover the deception. She will be to all purposes dead, and buried with her father. After it is all over, and the others are asleep (I shall manage to slip a little something into the wine that will be drunk after the business is concluded), you and I will steal down to the vault, open it, lift her out, seal the place, and then bear her to a house in the village where I have made preparations for her to be received."

" It certainly sounds simple."

" Nothing could be simpler! And as for the rest, all you will have to do will be to see that she does not escape from the house while I am gone. You can feign illness, so no one will wonder that you remain behind. I will hasten back to Milan with the others, make my report, claim the reward, and then, as soon as chance offers, escape from the city and return hither. You shall have your share of the money and can go where you will ; as for me, — well, that does not matter."

" Will you marry the girl ?" said the trooper, with a laugh.

"What is that to you?" cried von Ettergarde, with an angry oath, rising and striding toward the entrance to the tower.

So the wretched fate which the craft and dastardly cruelty of my former master had planned for his helpless captives was close at hand unless by some stroke of fortune we could intervene and thwart both his murderous designs and von Ettergarde's unscrupulous intentions. At the latter I was in no whit surprised, but the manifest cold-bloodedness of the Visconti's orders shocked me, and revealed to me how wrong I had been in allowing myself to think that my beloved and her father were in no immediate danger. What I had heard wrought an instant change in me. No longer was I troubled by the haunting dread with which I had so recently been assailed. The fact that dire danger menaced her in whom all my fondest hopes, all my dearest desires, were bound up roused my courage to its wonted pitch. It mattered not that I was not certain my passion was returned; this never for a breathing-space came into my mind. A deed was meditated for which the annals of our time, big with crime though they were, offered scarce a parallel. So long as I could stir a foot or lift a hand, I determined to strive to foil those who were to be the instruments of its accomplishment. For the time I put selfish motives entirely from my thought.

The trooper with whom von Ettergarde had been conversing still remained seated upon the bench muttering to himself, so Hartzheim and I were forced to withdraw to the bottom of the terrace with great caution. Reaching the spot where Berni was awaiting us, my friend suggested that we retire to a place where we could speak with more freedom; accordingly we went down again among the olives.

"Part of those men must be somehow lured from the entrance to the tower," said I. "Then if we make a sudden dash, perchance we can win the door, and that, if once won, might easily be held against all six."

"I think it can be managed," said

Hartzheim, "if our friend here will play his part as he agreed."

"You have but to tell me what you wish," said Berni, "and it shall be done."

"Good!" cried my friend. "This, then, strikes me as being the most feasible plan. After you have conducted us to the base of the terrace at the point yonder just opposite where the path from the village approaches, do you retrace your steps and take up your position somewhere near the path and not very far from the tower. There do you set up a great outcry for help as though you were being murdered, and shout, 'Von Ettergarde! von Ettergarde!' That is the name of the officer in command. It is more than likely that at least a part of the troopers will rush toward you, thinking you are one of their comrades, for two of their number have gone down to the lake and are undoubtedly expected back at any moment, though we have taken the necessary precautions to prevent their inopportune appearance. If you are successful in creating this little diversion, we shall not be slow in seizing upon the most favorable chance that offers, and in making a dash for the doorway of the tower."

"If the troopers of the Visconti were stone deaf, I would draw them away from the tower by my cries," exclaimed Berni, with a chuckle.

"Some of the village folk may be roused and come hither to complicate matters," said Hartzheim, "but we shall have to take that risk."

Berni now led us to the left over a piece of rough ground, and posted us where we were in no danger of being observed, but where, by lifting our heads, we could see everything that took place in front of the tower.

"You will not have long to wait," he said, as he left us.

I was heartily thankful for this assurance, since now that affairs were approaching a crisis I was exceedingly loath to lie supine in concealment. Hartzheim with his usual imperturbability crouched by my side, occasionally running his finger along the edge of his sword, as though to satisfy himself that it was in a fit condition to do good execution. One of the men who had been seated in the doorway of the tower had gone within. Presently he reappeared, bearing a flagon and some drinking-cups. These he distributed and proceeded to fill. The trooper who had agreed to assist von Ettergarde had joined the group, and all were evidently in the best of humor. Occasionally we could hear what was said, but most of their conversation failed to reach us. In the midst of their good cheer a piercing cry, as of some person in mortal agony, went up into the night. So sudden was it, so wild, so penetrating, that both Hartzheim and I, although we were expecting it, were thrilled and startled. Again it rose, and then there followed frantic appeals to von Ettergarde for aid. I raised myself upon one knee to mark the effect of this outburst upon the troopers. Their drinking-cups were cast aside, and, even as I watched, von Ettergarde and another, with their weapons drawn, rushed from the platform in the direction of the cries, while two of the others went as far as the edge of the terrace.

"Now!" exclaimed Hartzheim, in a whisper, and as he spoke we were upon our feet.

Being the more agile of the two, I darted in advance of my friend along the face of the tower. The wine-bearer, with the flagon still in his hand, was standing in the doorway, while on the lowest of the three steps which led to the entrance, his face set in the direction the troopers had taken, was a short, thickly-built man, whom I took to be the keeper. He was gripping the handle of his sword, and seemed to be on the point of joining the two soldiers at the edge of the terrace, when a pebble gritted under my foot. The sound caused him to turn his head, and he descried Hartzheim and myself not twenty feet distant. For an instant he appeared dazed, our garb deceiving him, then he uttered a cry that rivalled the one given by our ally and guide, and tried to interpose between me and the doorway. But his surprise and hesitation, although brief, enabled me to effect my end. I eluded the stroke he aimed at me, and charged full upon the man in the doorway, who had had no time to draw his weapon. He cast the flagon full at my head, and, as I stooped to avoid it, sprang back within the tower and whipped out his sword. As my blade met his I heard the clash of steel from without, and knew that Hartzheim had engaged the keeper.

A large torch stuck in a cranny shed a flickering light over the room which occupied almost the entire floor of the structure. In the centre of the rear wall was a cavernous fireplace; on the right of this, an open trap led to the cellar and vaults; and on the left there was a stair-way giving access to the rooms above. All this I took in at a glance as I bounded into the room. The man whom I encountered was no swordsman, a mere toy in my hands, and after a few passes I sent his weapon spinning in the air. He cringed before me, begging for mercy; and, though I knew it was no time for dallying and giving quarter, I had not the heart to take the poor wretch's life in cold blood.

"Down you go," said I, pointing to the open trap, "and be quick about it!"

He did not wait to be bidden a second time, and disappeared in speedy fashion, while I dropped the door above him and shot the bolt that held it into its socket. Two strides took me to the entrance to the tower, where a single look told me I was none too soon. At the foot of the steps the prostrate keeper was gasping his life out, while Hartzheim was beating off the blades of two troopers, and endeavor-in the meanwhile to retreat to the shelter of the doorway. As I sprang to the lower step and thrust at one of my friend's assailants, out of the gloom in the direction of the village leaped von Ettergarde and a fourth trooper.

"To the tower," cried Hartzheim, "but give them a taste of steel first."

We forced the two who faced us back a pace, Hartzheim inflicting a slight wound upon his antagonist, then we turned and gained the shelter of the doorway, wheeling about in time to meet the combined rush of the four, von Ettergarde at their head. For a few seconds the outcome seemed doubtful, but the doorway was narrow, and they found it difficult to reach us with their swords; so after a little they retreated to the bottom of the steps discomforted, two of them at least bearing evidence that our points had penetrated something besides leather. Von Ettergarde to my disgust came off unharmed, and was now disposed to parley.

"What do you want?" he demanded of Hartzheim, not condescending to notice me.

"A wise question," said my friend. "Why did you not inquire before? We have come to release your prisoners, which we shall do presently without so much as 'by your leave.'"

Von Ettergarde laughed.

"You are prisoners yourselves," said he. "You have run your necks into the noose."

"Of what use is the noose if you cannot tighten it? You tried just now. Perhaps you would like to try again."

Von Ettergarde made no reply, but whispered something in the ear of one of his men, who immediately set out in the direction of the village. I did not at all fancy the turn affairs had now taken, but my friend seemed unconcerned. For a moment or two nothing more was said, then upon this silence broke the not far distant ring of meeting steel, following upon which came a sharp cry of pain.

Von Ettergarde and his two companions glanced apprehensively at one another, while Hartzheim thrust his head out of the doorway, and cried in his great deep voice, —

"Ho, Leo Berni!"

There was an answering shout from the darkness, the sound of steps, and then the figure of our guide burst from the gloom. Now we were man for man. Down the steps sprang Hartzheim and I, but von Ettergarde and the two remaining troopers did not attempt to withstand our onset. Away they went as fast as their legs could carry them, over the edge of the terrace, crashing through the laurels, and disappearing into the murk of the night.

Berni was in high spirits as he joined us.

"I had a little dispute out yonder," said he, with a laugh. "Some hulking fellow came rushing along, and ordered me from the pathway. I objected to move, so we tried conclusions with our swords. I fear his spirit is ranging in another region now, though, hearing you shout, I did not pause to discover if he were sped. The thrust I gave him, however, when properly delivered, is one that carries death with it."

"Your encounter and your prompt response to my friend's call were most opportune," said I.

By this time we had reached the entrance to the tower.

"Von Ettergarde will try to rouse the villagers," said Hartzheim, "and there is need of the greatest haste. Berni and I will stand guard, Luigi, while you go above and release the prisoners."

I sheathed my sword, ran within, and plucked the torch from the cranny. With a heart fast throbbing I mounted the winding stairs. On either side of the narrow landing on the second floor was a rivet-clenched door chained and barred.

"Angela!" I cried; "Angela!"

The bare walls gave back my voice in cavernous reduplication, and it was impossible to tell if my appeal was answered, so I set myself to unfastening the chains and bolts which held the door communicating with the room on the outer face of the tower. Disappointment awaited my efforts. The place was empty. With all haste I fell to undoing the fastenings of the door opposite. As the barrier swung inward on creaking hinges, I caught up the torch, which I had leaned against the wall, and held it high above my head. The room was hung with dingy arras, and furnished with a slight show of comfort, but at the first glance I thought I was to be disappointed a second time. On looking closer, however, I caught sight of a figure kneeling with averted face as if in

prayer before a pallet in the corner.   I
took a step forward.

"Angela!" said I, tenderly.

The face of my beloved — for it was she
— was raised, surprise, hope, doubt, all
written upon it.   In the flaring torchlight
my features must have been indistinct, for
I saw fear leap into her eyes.   My trooper's dress, too, made recognition difficult.
I lowered the torch and advanced to the
centre of the room.

"Do you not know me, Signorina?"
said I.   "It is I, Luigi della Verria."

In an instant she was upon her feet.

"You!" she cried, shading her eyes
with her hand, and gazing at me as though
she could scarcely believe what she had
heard; "is it really you?   Oh, how I have
prayed that you would come!   Thank
God!   Thank God!"

She swayed as though she would fall,
and I sprang to her side, casting the torch
upon the floor.   As I took her in my
arms our eyes met in the dim light, and I
read in hers that which thrilled my whole
being with rapture.   There was no need

of words of wooing. Words could wait. Each knew what the other's heart held, and that sufficed. Scribes who write learnedly of love, putting words of ardor into the wooer's mouth, at crucial times like this, have no knowledge of such intense feeling as those moments of silence held for my beloved and me.

" There was no need of words of wooing." — Page 308

Chapter XX

The Flight by Night

IT was Angela who first returned to earth from our vision of paradise.

"My father!" she exclaimed, as she disengaged herself from my arms, "have you found him?"

"No," I answered.

"Come," she said, "let us go to him. He is in one of the rooms above."

Lifting the torch from the floor, I led the way to the landing overhead, and soon father and daughter were clasped in a fond embrace. How it was between Angela and myself Signor Canaro must have surmised, for he said to me,—

"Had I a son, he could not have done more than you have done, Signor della Verria."

"It is to my friend below," I replied, "to whom thanks are chiefly due. I could have accomplished nothing without his advice and aid. But further danger may threaten, so let us be gone."

I was rejoiced to learn that Signor Canaro's wound gave him but little inconvenience, for I now saw no obstacle to prevent our speedy flight. I found on descending that nothing new had developed during my absence, and after I had presented my beloved and her father to Hartzheim and Berni, and they had expressed in the warmest terms their gratitude for our efforts in their behalf (Angela endearing herself to me all the more by the feeling manner in which she addressed Hartzheim, thereby completely winning his heart), I proposed that we quit the tower.

"The sooner the better," said Berni, "else will it be no easy matter to gain the lake without an encounter."

A joy which I will not try to describe filled me as I walked by Angela's side, assisting her when the way was rough, whispering to her words of encouragement and love. Her spirits rose with a bound after we lost sight of the dismal walls which had been her prison, and as we trod hand in hand through the night, to both of us (despite the gloom) the path seemed one illumined by a light fairer than any our eyes had ever before looked upon.

It was necessary to return as we had come, and as we threaded the dark lanes of the village of Vezio, we noticed a growing commotion in the main thoroughfare, shouts and the flaring of torches. Von Ettergarde was rousing the villagers.

Though Signor Canaro seemed apprehensive, Angela appeared to have no fear of recapture, and I was buoyed up by her confidence, though otherwise I believe I should have shared her father's anxiety; for the noise swelled behind us, and as we reached the point where the pathway began to pitch sharply toward the lake, we descried several torch-bearers hurrying after us.

"They cannot have seen us," said Berni, "and I doubt if they follow us at once.   They will think to intercept us, should we come this way, a few paces back where another path joins the one we are following.   It will hardly occur to them that we have already passed."

Our guïde's conjecture was reassuring, and proved to be correct ; this was providential, as our progress was of necessity slow, owing to the perils of the pathway. Berni led the party, I close after him, ever ready to aid Angela, who came next, then followed her father, and finally Hartzheim. Without accident we reached the valley of the Esino, and soon were hastening along the level ground to where our boat was moored.   It was not difficult to see that a storm was impending.   The gloom had thickened, and not a breath of air stirred upon the surface of the lake.

When we reached the boat, we found but one of the sailors in charge of her.

" Where are your comrades ? " cried I, in astonishment.

" They did not expect you for some time yet," answered the man, reluctantly, " but they are not far away."

"At one of the wine-houses, I suppose!" exclaimed Hartzheim, in a furious rage. "Well, pack yourself off and summon them, and if you are not back quickly, you may look to find your boat gone."

The man sped away in the direction of the nearest light, while Hartzheim and I, outwardly calm, but furious with concealed anger, raised the two troopers whom we had left in the prow of the boat and bestowed them by the side of the pile of provisions upon the quay. I fear, in our impatience, we handled them with scant consideration, but after all a few bruises are but a small matter. Doubtless they counted themselves fortunate to get off so lightly.

While Hartzheim was loosening the mooring-rope, I moved toward Angela, who was standing by her father's side. She came to meet me, divining by her fine instinct what was passing in my mind.

"Do not put blame upon the sailors when they come," she said. "They are

our only means of escape, and what should
we do if you should anger them and they
should refuse to help us?"

I saw that she was right, and turned
to caution Hartzheim, who, I knew, would
be likely to use a sharp tongue unless
warned.

"The Signorina is wise," said my
friend. "I will hold my peace, though
it will not be an easy matter."

Very soon the delinquents came dashing
up, their leader profuse in his apologies.
We were so gratified to find that the men
were all of them in possession of their
senses, and not stupefied by the fumes of
drink, as we had expected they would be,
that we were able to accept their excuses
with some show of indulgence.

We now bade farewell to Leo Berni,
from whom we parted with real regret; he
in turn declaring that were it not for saying good by to his people he should be
inclined to cast his lot with us. As we
were about to embark, Signor Canaro
pressed upon the valiant trooper a ring
heavy with gems, which he begged him to

wear in remembrance of him and of his daughter.

As we drew out from shore, the lightning began to play behind the crest of a lofty peak on the further side of the lake which the sailors called Monte Crocione.

"It is better to be here in the storm than there," said Angela to me, as we sat side by side in the stern.

I glanced back in the direction which she indicated, and saw the flash of moving lights all along the mountain slope. Von Ettergarde had been abundantly successful in rousing the villagers of Vezio, but he had evidently not been keen enough to surmise that we had had a guide to whom the paths leading from the tower had, from boyhood, been familiar ground.

We had told the boatmen we were likely to be pursued, but I saw by the way they bent to their oars, and by the apprehensive glances they cast at the sky when a lightning flash lit up the brooding expanse of water, that it was not for fear of being overtaken that they were pulling so lustily.

" Is there danger from the storm ? " I asked of the one nearest us.

" That there is, Signore," said he. " We should never have ventured out had it not been that we promised you our assistance."

" Can we not seek some shelter till the tempest passes? " said I.

" We are striving to reach a place of safety," he answered, " a little cove that is half cave on the eastern side of the Bellaggio promontory. We shall be quite out of danger there, and dry."

It was really a race with the storm that our boatmen were rowing. Little puffs of warm air fanned our cheeks, then there was a perfect calm again. The thunder-growl momently became more threatening; the mountains seemed to rock upon their very foundations, and the heavens to vibrate above us. Our boat shot through the water faster than I deemed it possible for so clumsy a craft. I could hear the labored breathing of the boatmen, who never for a second relaxed their efforts. Already the Val d'Esino and the Tower of Vezio were left far behind. The lights upon the mountain slope faded into faint points, and then were wholly lost. One instant it was as though we were moving forward through a void of limitless night in which no planet ever shone; the next we were enveloped in a sheet of dazzling flame.

Though I had never before experienced such an aërial display, I felt no concern for myself; but for Angela I was full of anxiety. She must have read this on my face by the light of one of the flashes, for she said, —

"I fear nothing now, Luigi. Nature has always been my friend."

She had never called me Luigi before, and the thrill I experienced on hearing my name upon her lips caused me so wholly to forget our surroundings that I needs must take her in my arms for a moment despite the fact that the lightning was likely at any instant to betray me to the eyes of the sailors, to those of my friend, and of Angela's father.

Erelong there was a gust of cool air, and a few large drops of rain fell. Then a forked flame shot from the sky, and a sound as of the rending of the universe smote our ears. Somewhere upon the promontory toward which we were speeding the bolt struck, and the nearness of our haven of refuge was revealed to us. I heard the leader of the sailors give a sharp word of command, whereat the men ceased rowing and rested on their oars. The pause was but momentary, however, for when another flash came they resumed their stroke. Soon we were close to the shore, and just before the flood of the storm was loosened, still aided by the fitful light in the heaven, we glided into a little cove over which a shelf of rock impended, and above which the cliff rose sheer to the height of one hundred feet. As we were on the leeward side of the promontory, the tempest driving up the lake from the southwest, our shelter was both secure and dry.

How long we were forced to remain here I cannot say. Safe for a while from pursuit, protected from the rage of the elements, with the one in all the world dearest to me by my side, I gave little heed to the lapse of time, to the roaring of the wind, and the deluge of the rain. Even after there came a rift in the rack it seemed unwise to proceed at once, owing to the roughness of the water and the force of the gale, but toward morning, just as the first faint glimmering of dawn showed between the mountain crests, we put out and began coasting the western shore. Soon after sunrise the water grew calmer, for we had left behind the central track of the storm, and as the breeze now shifted to the north, the oars were unshipped and the sail hoisted.

We reached Lecco considerably before noon, and found Galbo, all preparations for our journey made, awaiting us. After a brief tarry for rest and refreshment we mounted. The horses were in fine fettle, the sky was without a wisp of cloud, the air was cool and fresh, and with hearts elate we rode out of the mountain country through the rolling foot-hills to Bergamo, where we lay for the night. We should have pressed forward another ten miles to Grumello had we not had Signor Canaro's condition to consider; but we soon discovered that it would be necessary for him to husband his strength with the greatest care, and hence shortened the distance we had planned to compass on leaving Lecco.

On the following morning I had my first opportunity to broach to Signor Canaro that which was now the dearest desire of my life, my marriage to Angela. He received my proposal with all the kindness and gentle courtesy which marked his nature, and even before I told him what my prospects were (that I was the heir to my cousin Alberto Gambacorta of Padua), he yielded his hearty assent. What his words were I will not repeat lest I seem to set forth my own praise unduly. It will suffice to state that his reception of me in my new attitude straightway transported me to a perfect heaven of bliss, and I was about to wheel Hawkwood to Angela's side to whisper to her how I had won her father's approval, and see the blush-rose dye her cheek, when Signor Canaro detained me by saying, —

"She will not be a dowerless bride, Signor della Verria, though I must perforce leave to the Visconti the bulk of my possessions. When I was persecuted by Gian Galeazzo's uncle, Bernabo, I converted a portion of my property into jewels. These we shall be able to carry with us when we leave Brescia."

This was the first intimation I had had that Signor Canaro expected to visit his home even for the briefest period. Hartzheim and I had discussed the matter that morning before our departure from Bergamo, and had decided that it would be the part of wisdom to avoid Brescia entirely, but I now realized that Signor Canaro would never consent to this; and, after all, a short halt there might lead to no harm. Although von Ettergarde would lose no time in acquainting the Visconti with the escape of his captives, and although my former master would naturally hit on Brescia as the spot where he might most naturally re-cage the flown prisoners, it did not seem to me possible that his emissaries could overtake us unless we had the misfortune to be detained a considerable number of hours.

After consulting with Hartzheim, we decided to change slightly our former plan so as to allow for a brief tarry at Brescia. Our route to Padua lay by way of Mantua, — a wide detour, it is true, but Verona and the adjacent country was little less than an armed and hostile camp.

Chapter XXI

The House of the Canari

AS we were drawing near Brescia that afternoon, I left Angela, by whose side I had been riding, and joined her father, noticing that he seemed fatigued and dejected, Hartzheim taking my place near my betrothed. Signor Canaro said nothing for several moments after I asked him how he fared, but kept his eyes fixed upon the distance out of which rose dimly the towers of the city which had for centuries been the home of his race.

"I believe it is not the wound that drags me down," he answered finally, "but the knowledge that I must flee before that viper who has drawn his coils about so much of our fair land of northern Italy, who will one day, if I mistake not, encompass many another prosperous city to the ruin of its rulers and its leading men ; the knowledge that he will sweep into his coffers well-nigh all that is by birthright mine, and I am powerless to avert it."

"You have never told me," said I, "how he dares to wrong you so."

"He has a pretended claim, else even in his position, all-powerful though he apparently deems it, he would hardly venture to employ such extreme measures. I had intended to explain the whole matter to you, and perhaps there is no better time than now.

"You are in a measure acquainted with the persecutions which my daughter and I endured at the hands of Bernabo Visconti, so you may imagine with what joy I welcomed the news of his downfall. All that I had heard of Gian Galeazzo before his deposal of his uncle prepossessed me in his favor, and while Brescia was among the last of Bernabo's possessions to yield to the new lord, I proclaimed myself in his favor at the outset. I cannot recall exactly when I first had a personal communication from him, but I should say about a month ago. In it he bade me wait upon him in Milan as soon as it was convenient for me to do so, as he had matters of special importance to discuss with me. Thinking he referred to municipal affairs, in which, with the change of power, I had taken considerable interest, I replied, stating when I would present myself at his palace. I was delayed in leaving Brescia—"

"Ah," I interposed, "perhaps that is why I was made the bearer of a missive to you. I think I have never told you that the day after your departure for Milan I called upon you to deliver a letter from Gian Galeazzo."

"The Visconti informed me at our first meeting that he had summoned me a second time, but of course I did not know through whom. The delay of which I spoke was but of brief duration. Angela, who had never visited Milan, begged that she might accompany me, and I was only too glad of her companionship, never dreaming that I was leading her into peril. We made the journey without incident and were soon established in lodgings recommended to us by Brescia friends. I hastened, on the morning following my arrival, to the palace of the Visconti, and was graciously received by him, but it was not till toward the close of our interview that there dawned upon me the faintest notion of what that master of craft really desired of me. 'There are certain papers,' he said casually, after there had been much talk concerning the condition of affairs in Brescia, 'which I wish to discuss with you if you will kindly give me an hour of your time on the morrow.' 'Papers?' I replied, with some surprise. 'Yes,' he returned, 'documents which recently came to my hand quite accidentally while I chanced to be disposing of some of my uncle's effects.'

"At the mention of his uncle a sense of an impending unpleasant disclosure seized me, though I did not dream how vitally I was to be affected thereby. 'The writings,' said he, 'are by no means of recent date, in fact they were executed about the time my ancestor, Azzone, became the Overlord of Brescia.' At this a swift suspicion smote me. 'May I ask,' I said, 'if these writings concern me personally?' 'Filippo Canaro was your grandfather, was he not?' the Visconti asked. 'He was,' I replied. 'Then,' said the Lord of Milan, 'it is my opinion, inasmuch as you, through your father, are Filippo Canaro's heir, that the papers very decidedly concern you. In them are embodied certain agreements which apparently have been only partially fulfilled,— but we will speak of these matters when we meet again,' and I was dismissed with the request, which was virtually a command, that I repair to the palace at a certain hour the next day.

"I was familiar enough with the history of my family at the time of the downfall of the Brusati in Brescia. I knew that my grandfather had opposed Azzone Visconti, and, when that prince had triumphed, had purchased exemption

from exile at the sacrifice of almost everything he possessed. I was morally certain
that Gian Galeazzo had no claim upon
my family that had not been satisfied
long since. The papers, the documents,
which the Lord of Milan asserted that
he possessed were doubtless forgeries executed by his uncle, just before his deposal,
as a final means of bending me to his
ends.

"Naturally I was much disquieted by
the Visconti's revelation, but I hoped to
be able to prove to his satisfaction the
falsity of the writings, and the injustice of
pressing such a claim. I had yet to discover the real nature of the man with
whom I had to deal. Seeking the palace
at the appointed hour on the following
day, I was informed that his Lordship
could not see me. Another time of meeting was set, and again I failed to obtain
the expected interview. I began to realize
that I was like a bird, about whom the net
which is to prove its undoing is gradually
being closer and closer drawn.

"At length, late in the afternoon of

that memorable day when you rendered me such timely assistance, I succeeded in gaining the Visconti's presence, and it was not long before I saw beneath that suave and fair-seeming exterior the fangs of the venomous viper.   He was satisfied, he said, that the ancient claims against the Canaro estate were still outstanding, and despite what I affirmed in regard to my ability to disprove this statement, he hinted to me that, unless I complied with his wishes to the letter (this I speedily . discovered meant beggary), grave consequences might ensue.   In either case, whether I bowed to his will or not, I knew myself ruined.   I looked upon the blandly smiling face before me, and a great contempt that changed to a great anger rose within me.   I tossed prudence to the winds.   I set before him in plain words what he proposed doing.   I drew him a vivid picture of his own cowardly and despicable nature, and finally I cursed him and his whole viper brood.   Toward the last he became fearful for his safety, and summoned some attendants, who ejected me from his presence. I went forth dazed with rage, and had hardly become master of myself when his hirelings set upon me in the Via San Lorenzo."

The recollection of all he had suffered at the hands of my former master so moved Signor Canaro that every vestige of color left his face, and for an instant I feared that he would lose his seat in the saddle; but he recovered himself, and we rode for a space in silence, for what consolation could I offer to one who had suffered such grievous wrong?

Hartzheim broke in upon our meditation by suggesting a moment's halt for consultation, inasmuch as we were now approaching the city walls.

"I understand," he said, addressing Signor Canaro, "that it is your desire to pause for a brief space at your home. It strikes me that it would be unwise for all of us to accompany you, provided a different and satisfactory arrangement can be made, since we do not wish, if we can avoid it, to leave behind us any sign of our tarry here. By this time to-morrow I trust we shall be beyond the Visconti's power, but I doubt if we can win farther than Montechiaro to-night, and it would be most unfortunate if pur-suers should get track of us, and over-take us there, as they might be able to do should we give them the means of tracing us."

"There is a reputable inn just without the Porta Venezia where you, Angela, and Galbo might await Signor della Verria and myself," answered Signor Canaro.

"Just the spot," said Hartzheim. "Even should we be tracked thither, those pursuing would naturally infer that we had ridden toward Verona."

So it was decided that I should accom-pany Signor Canaro into the city, while the others, by making a considerable de-tour, should avoid the town, gain the shelter of the inn, and there abide our coming. Bidding Angela be of good cheer, we dismounted, gave our horses into the charge of Hartzheim and Galbo, and strode toward the gateway, Signor Canaro half muffling his face in his cloak to avoid any chance recognition.

Unaccosted and unheeded we gained the house of the Canari. While we stood awaiting the servant in whose charge the palace had been left, I marked the pallor of my companion's face, but as I was uncertain whether it was owing to exhaustion or to the strong emotion naturally due to the thought that he might be entering for the last time his own home and that of his fathers, I refrained from commenting upon it, though it gave me no little anxiety. But the old retainer who threw open the door was not silent. He took instant fright at the almost death-like countenance of his master.

" Signore, Signore," he cried. " What has happened ? Has ill befallen the Signorina ? "

" No, no, Tonio ; thank heaven, not that ! " said Signor Canaro.

" Will you come with me ? " he asked, as we passed within.

Thinking that he might prefer to be alone, and had only invited me to accompany him out of courtesy, I declined, saying I would remain with Tonio. Assuring me that he would not keep me long waiting, he crossed the courtyard and was lost to view. As I watched him, and noted the uncertainty of his steps, I regretted that I had declined to go with him.

"What ails the master, Signore?" said the wondering servant.

"He has been ill," I returned, knowing it would be unwise to arouse the man's curiosity by telling him Signor Canaro had been wounded; "moreover, he has ridden far to-day, and is much fatigued."

"And will he not bide at home now that he is here?"

"No; he is obliged to go at once upon another journey."

The man was bewildered, but he showed that he knew his place by forbearing to question me further.

I began pacing up and down the courtyard, listening anxiously to catch the first sound of Signor Canaro's returning footsteps. The moments slipped by, and at length I grew uneasy. I reflected that Angela's father had told me he would not keep me long waiting. Again and again my eyes sought the stairway which he had ascended. Tonio, too, showed that he shared my anxiety. At length I could endure the suspense no longer.

"Something may have happened to your master," said I.

"Shall we go and see, Signore?" asked the man.

"Yes," said I; "do you lead the way."

In haste we mounted to the second floor.

"He would hardly be here," said I. "Where are the apartments which he usually occupies?"

"On the floor above, Signore."

When we reached the next landing we paused.

"Signor Canaro," I called.

There was no answer. Again I called, much louder than before, and still there was no reply.

I chanced to glance at Tonio, and saw apprehension and fear plainly written on his face.

"What has happened, Signore?" said
he, his voice unconsciously falling to a
whisper.

"We must see," said I; "which are
your master's apartments?"

"Yonder," he answered, pointing to a
half-open door at the extremity of the
corridor, toward which I strode with feel-
ings of the greatest concern, Tonio hanging back as though he dreaded what might
be revealed.

I halted upon the threshold and pushed
wide the door. The room was small and
richly furnished. On two sides were
couches after the Byzantine fashion.
Heavy draperies hid the walls. An inlaid cabinet stood in one corner, and in
the centre of the apartment there was a
curious table,—a slab of lapis lazuli sup-
ported by four bronze griffins. I thought
the room empty, and was crossing toward
the doorway at right angles to the one by
which I had entered, when I noticed that
one of the couches had been slightly
moved and that at the farther end the
arras hung as though some object broke

its symmetrical folds.   Hastening to the spot, I drew back the hangings, and there lay the body of Signor Canaro before an open sliding panel which disclosed a small metallic casket.

As my eyes fell upon the ghastly grayness of his countenance, a momentary panic seized me, and I looked down upon him in speechless horror.   It seemed to me that he must be dead.   One hand was outflung toward me, and presently, when I had recovered a little from the shock, I bent over and touched him.   There was a feeble fluttering at the wrist, like a faint flickering watch-fire seen by a wanderer in the dark, which revived hope and made me quite myself again.   With a shout I summoned Tonio.   Together we lifted the swooned man, placed him on one of the couches, and set about restoring him to consciousness.   This we finally succeeded in doing, but so weak was he that he could scarcely raise his head, and the words that fell from his lips were hardly articulate.   I drew Tonio to one side.

" Is there a physician near ? " said I.

"Yes, Signore; the one who usually attends the master lives in the next street."

"Do you summon him," said I, "and be quick. Fetch another, should you not find the one you seek at home."

Tonio gone, I seated myself at Signor Canaro's side, moistening his lips occasionally with a few drops of strong Calabrian wine, watching eagerly for some sign of returning strength in his pallid countenance. Occasionally he opened his eyes and let them rest for an instant on mine, then closed them again without attempting to speak. There was a strong appeal in his look, yet he would not put into words that for which his heart clamored. I was not slow to divine his desire, and could not steel myself to deny him, however much compliance pained me. Signor Canaro believed himself to be dying, and yearned for the presence of his daughter.

Delay in the house of the Canari meant the direst danger to us all. Every hour, every fraction of an hour, brought nearer those whom I knew the Visconti, in rage at the frustration of his schemes, had despatched in search of us. Yet what could be done? Fortune, who had showered her favors upon us thus far, had suddenly deserted us, and an evil fate (in the person of the Great Viper) seemed about to enmesh us in its coils.

Again Signor Canaro unclosed his eyes and fastened upon me that appealing look. I nodded my head.

"Yes," I said, "as soon as Tonio returns she shall be sent for."

A more restful expression now settled upon his face, but the color did not return, nor did his pulse perceptibly strengthen. Some vital breath must soon fan the flame of life, else it would expire and leave but ashes.

At length there was the sound of footsteps on the stair, and I hastened to the doorway to greet Tonio and the man of healing.

"I could not find the master's physician," the servant said, "so I have brought one whose cures are famous beyond Brescia, though he is scorned by those of the schools."

"Alessandro Muzio, at your service, Signore," said the man in question, whom I saw by his garb and air to be one of those who brood by night over the mysteries of the stars, who interpret the strange workings of the earth, and are said (how truly I know not) to hold communion with disembodied souls, and with the dark spirits of a nether sphere.

A great shock of hair like a horse's forelock escaped from his conical hat and hid his brow. A dark beard, thickly sprinkled with gray, grew high upon his cheeks, hiding his mouth, and falling to his breast. It was the eyes that gave character to the face. Deep set, and seemingly as changeable as a chameleon in the sun, now they slumbered like a dull coal, now they glowed and sparkled with an intense light. A single garment of some blue Eastern fabric girt by a silken cord hid his ample figure, and lent a certain majesty to his bearing. Though I realized that among many there was an unfavorable feeling toward such as he, I could not avoid being strongly impressed by him.

"You will find your patient yonder," I said, pointing to the couch where Signor Canaro lay.

The leech bowed and entered the room, while I remained in the corridor for a word with Tonio.

"You know an inn outside the Porta Venezia?" I asked.

"Yes, Signore, the inn of the Three Kings.   It is so called because—"

"Never mind about that, but listen to what I have to say."

"Yes, Signore."

"I wish you to hasten as fast as may be to this inn, and inquire there for Signor Hartzheim. To him you are to say that you have come at my orders to conduct him and Signorina Canaro hither. Should he not be disposed to believe you, bid him call the Signorina, but do not under any circumstances so forget yourself as to alarm her needlessly in regard to the condition of her father. He may be much recovered by the time you return. Say, if you are questioned, that I will explain everything on their arrival."

I descended with Tonio to the street entrance, and, having seen him start at a brisk pace upon his mission, secured the door and again mounted the stairs. I found the leech, or seer, awaiting me in the corridor just outside the room where Signor Canaro lay. He put to me a few searching inquiries, and then drew from beneath his robe a thin and worn leather case from which he took a slender vial containing a liquid that sparkled like molten gold.

"The Signore is exhausted," he said, "nervously and physically, and needs complete rest."

" I feared that it might be worse," said I, "but that is bad enough. We should be gone out of Brescia within the hour."

" So I gathered from what the Signore said. I would fain work a miracle, but that is not in my power; yet this I can promise you : if three drops of this " (holding up the vial) " be administered on the stroke of every hour, by midnight the Signore will be able to continue his journey."

" Pray heaven it may not then be too late !" I exclaimed, as we passed into the room together.

The apartment adjoining the one where the sick man was reclining was a library, or study ; beyond this was a bedchamber, and thither we bore Signor Canaro. When he was comfortably bestowed, and a first potion from the vial administered, I had the satisfaction of seeing him drop into a profound slumber. The man of mysteries and healing now gave me minute directions, which he admonished me must be scrupulously followed, and having presented to him his fee and, accompanied him to the palace entrance, I returned to Signor Canaro's bedside, having first taken care to secure the metallic casket from its place of concealment behind the arras. This I placed so that Signor Canaro's eyes would rest upon it when he unclosed them, and then seated myself to await the summons which should announce the arrival of Hartzheim and my beloved.

Chapter XXII

Out of the Viper's Coils

IT lacked but little of the stroke of midnight. In the silver lustre near the door a single taper showed a greenish-yellow flame. On the couch where Signor Canaro had reclined that afternoon my friend Hartzheim was breathing heavily in slumber. Within, by her father's bed-side, Angela, the flower of my heart, watched like a white spirit. Through all the house of the Canari there brooded a great silence.

It was my watch, and I needs must move frequently to keep awake. Now I crept in to whisper some comforting word to Angela, now I peered into the garden from the darkness of the library, watching the indistinct and ghostly movements of the boughs of the limes that were by fits breeze-tossed; now I stole into the corridor and listened. It was here that I came most frequently and tarried longest. If the sound rose which I dreaded to hear, — the summons of armed men below, — I must catch its first echo.

Tonio had been dismissed for the night. This had been done after a consultation between Hartzheim and myself. We thought it best to let it appear that the house was entirely deserted. Should the emissaries of the Visconti arrive and demand admission, we decided to pay no heed to them. Possibly they might retire without forcing an entrance, and in case they did use force the presence of a servant might lead to our discovery. He might be found, and frightened or tortured into revealing something. As for ourselves, we had made no plans. Signor Canaro was not in a condition to be consulted, and we did not wish to disturb Angela, who spent her every moment by her father's side, unless occasion forced us to do so

"There must be some place of concealment in all this huge house, whither we
can retire if we find ourselves caged,"
Hartzheim had said, when we talked the
matter over shortly after his arrival; so I
had tried to put worry away from me,
and to think, even if the dreaded men-at-
arms of the Visconti arrived, we might
somehow contrive to elude them.

I had just come from a whispered word
with Angela, and had left her father sleeping peacefully, the change that had taken
place in him since that afternoon being a
marvel to us all. His countenance had
lost the death-like cast, and when he was
roused, as had been directed, that the
medicine might be administered, his voice
was strong, his eye clear, and his hand
steady. It had been decided between my
betrothed and myself that should he still
be slumbering when midnight struck we
would waken him, for we had every confidence that he would be able to endure, at
least for a considerable number of hours,
the fatigues of our flight.

For several moments I stood in the

doorway which opened into the corridor, waiting as eagerly as ever man waited to catch the first peal that should herald the birth of another day. Never had time seemed so leaden-footed as now. I was telling myself that the next instant my ears must surely be gladdened by the welcome sound, when there rang through the hallways and corridors of the palace, faintly at first, then louder and more loud, not the midnight chime of bells, but the summons for admission from below.

I had fully made up my mind what I should do in case of this dreaded emergency. With a bound I sprang through the library into the room where Angela and her father were. My beloved had heard the noise and had risen to meet me.

"They have come," said I. "Rouse your father and await us here. My friend and I will go to reconnoitre. We shall soon return."

I found Hartzheim in the corridor doorway. Plucking a taper from the lustre, and lighting it, I hurried as swiftly and silently as possible toward the front of the palace, my friend at my side. We were not long in gaining a room which overlooked the street, where we loosened the casement and were able, without danger of detection, to view the scene below. A great flare of torches in the hands of a dozen city watchmen illumined the highway, which was blocked by a score of troopers, some on foot and some on horseback.

"Open!" we heard a voice shout, as the thunderous knocking ceased for an instant, "open in the name of the Lord of Milan and of Brescia!"

The man who demanded admission was Otto von Ettergarde.

We had seen enough, and we speedily retraced our steps. As we passed the head of the stairway, the noise grew more threatening, and we surmised that they had begun to batter in the doors. At the extremity of the corridor Angela and Signor Canaro were awaiting us, the latter erect and animated.

"We are surrounded," he said; "for we have just noted from the library window

the light of torches in the laneway beyond
the garden. We are not yet taken, however," he continued, "nor are we likely
to be at once unless those noisy fellows
without have sharper eyes than I give them
credit for. Come; I will show you where
we can conceal ourselves."

We followed Signor Canaro into the
library, and watched him swing out and
back a case, which was apparently built
into the wall, containing a rare collection
of illuminated missals. In the opening
thus revealed was a narrow door which
readily yielded to the pressure of the
hand, and showed a small recess from
which a staircase ascended.

"The door in the apartment above is
as cunningly hidden as this," said Signor
Canaro. "We can remain here until
they tire of searching for us, and then
perhaps, even though they leave the
house watched and guarded, contrive to
escape."

We took care to close the doors of the
rooms we had occupied, and to put everything to rights so that the apartments

should not seem to have been recently in use, then we entered the recess and became for the time being voluntary prisoners. Presently we heard sounds of the search for us, the tramping of heavy feet, the murmur of voices, then these noises grew indistinct, after a space to increase again in volume. Angela and I sat midway upon the staircase, below us Signor Canaro and Hartzheim. Despite the great peril in which we were placed, those hours of waiting and anxiety were full of a deep sweetness to me. Had I not by my side to kiss and to caress at will the one peerless maiden from the human flower-garden of the whole world? Could I not pour into her ear pictures of our love-life when we should have escaped out of the Viper's coils, and listen in return to her words of gratitude and praise for what I had already done, and to her expressions of confidence in what I was yet to do, for her and for her father?

At length all sounds without died entirely away, yet we did not deem it wise to venture forth. More than three hours

must have elapsed before it was decided that a move should be made. If
watchers had been set we wished to give
them time to become drowsy. Slowly and
noiselessly the case containing the missals
was swung outward, and Hartzheim and I
slipped from the recess into the library.
The faint gray light of dawn had begun
to steal into the room, and as my friend
crept toward the corridor I advanced to
the window, thinking perhaps I might be
able to see if any guards had been posted
in the garden. To my surprise — for I had
not been able to note the fact in the darkness, nor did I recall having observed it
on my first visit to the house of the Canari
— I discovered a balcony just outside the
window. Cautiously opening the casement, I stepped out and peered below, but
could see no one. Then I let my eye
follow the line of the palace to the left,
and found, to my inexpressible delight,
that both the adjoining house and the one
next it were supplied with balconies similar to the one upon which I was standing.
Here was a possible means of escape, if

the space between the balconies could be bridged. Hugging the wall, and tiptoeing along, I came to the edge of the gap. It was not more than seven feet from railing to railing.

"One of the Byzantine couches in the room adjoining the library will be just the thing!" I thought.

Back I crept as hastily as I dared. Angela and her father had emerged from our place of concealment, and to them in a whisper I confided my plan.

"The very thing," cried Signor Canaro, "dullard that I am that it did not occur to me! The second house is unoccupied, and from the grounds at the rear there is access to a side street which is not likely to be watched."

My heart gave a great bound of exultation at this news. As the gloom of night was beginning to lift, so was it with the darkness that had, for a space, beclouded our fortunes.

At this moment Hartzheim reappeared.

"There is a guard at the top of the stairway," said he, "and I think I heard some one stirring in the corridor on the right."

Hurriedly I told him of our plan.

"Bravo!" he cried, in a whisper, his face brightening; "we shall triumph over the Viper, after all."

Angela and her father retired, at our suggestion, behind the missal case, until we should have put our improvised bridge in position, then Hartzheim and I seized upon one of the couches. It was rather a cumbersome affair, by no means easy to handle, and we found that it was impossible to move it without making some noise. As we were preparing to pass it through the library casement, the sound of footfalls reached us from the corridor, light yet unmistakable. We set down our burden, and I started as though I would go toward the door.

"No," said Hartzheim, in a suppressed tone, "there should be but one of us. Leave it to me."

He slipped off his sword and drew a stiletto from his doublet, a weapon which I knew he detested, and which I had never before seen in his hand. I hardly recognized his face as he glided by me, the usual kindly look having quite gone out of it, and a hard and fierce resolve settled there in its stead. I realized that it was no hour for mercy. He into whose clutches we should fall, if captured, would show as little pity as the venomous reptile emblazoned on his ensign, or as the gaunt gray wolf of the Apennines. Yet I could not think of the man who was stealing along the corridor without a qualm. He as little dreamed of the swift death that lay in wait for him as does the lusty reveler when Hate, in the guise of Friendship, presses the poisoned cup to his lip.

Suddenly from the adjoining room came the noise of scuffling feet, then a dull blow and a spasmodic sound like the swift indrawing of breath. Presently I saw my friend's face again. It was still stern and set. He refastened his sword and seized upon the couch with eager energy.

" It had to be," he said, "and I was the one to do it, yet I like it not, least of

all in that way.   I trust there will be no
others, unless—" he stopped.

"Unless?" I repeated.

"Well, there is one among them for
whom a good honest thrust would be
far too saintly a speeding," he returned,
and I knew he referred to the man who
had been the Visconti's chief instrument
in the whole affair.

We were in constant fear lest a noise
should attract attention, and proceeded
with the utmost caution; consequently it
was some time before we had the couch
in position. The outcome of our efforts
was even more successful than I anticipated, and we hastened to summon my
betrothed and her father. Hartzheim was
the first to cross, then followed Signor
Canaro, and then Angela, my friend and
I each giving her a hand to steady her.
I was on the point of joining them,
when I bethought me of my cloak which I
had cast over a chair in the library that
I might not be hindered by its folds. Telling my companions what I sought, I sped
on tiptoe along the balcony to the open

casement, entered, had lifted my cloak, and was about retracing my steps when a footfall caused me to pause.

Before I had a chance to conceal myself a man strode into the room from the direction of the corridor. For a few seconds we stared at one another through the still indistinct light of dawn. Then at the same instant recognition came to both of us. The man was Otto von Ettergarde.

"Ah," said he, "'tis Signor Tallow-Locks!" using the same insulting epithet he had applied to me at our first meeting in the palace courtyard at Pavia. "This time there seems to be no one here to interrupt us," and he swiftly closed the door through which he had come, glanced into the bedchamber adjoining, and closed that door. I, in the meanwhile, had unsheathed my sword and swung the hangings fully free from the casement.

How von Ettergarde had chanced thus to come in upon me I could not imagine, but here he was, and I must face him. I felt, however, no sinking of the heart as he came forward; on the contrary, I was as calm as though I was about to engage in a friendly fencing bout. Life and love were at stake, aye, more! the lives of those to whom I was linked by the strongest ties of affection might hang upon the outcome, and yet I was unmoved. Von Ettergarde, on his part, was perfectly confident, and the fire that leaped from his cold and cruel eyes as our blades crossed might at any other time have made me feel that I had met more than my match.

At first my enemy, such was his complete assurance, made a pretence of playing with me, but seeing that I was not to be thrown off my guard, nor led to take advantage of his seeming carelessness, he tried to force me into a corner near the casement where my arm movement would be restricted, and he would have me at a serious disadvantage. I held my ground tenaciously, however, not giving back an inch, whereupon he retreated as though inviting me to attack. I suspected a ruse, and advanced with the greatest caution. Well was it that I did so, for with a sudden shifting of position he feinted and thrust so swiftly that it was not skill but a blind instinct which saved me. Of small avail my shirt of linked mail would have been in staying the force of that furious blow. His point was aimed straight at my heart, and I managed to turn it so that it passed between my arm and side, doing no more damage than to tear a great hole in my doublet. It was a stroke of which I had heard the famous *maître d'armes*, Houdon Despagnac, speak one evening in Bologna. Later the same night I had seen him illustrate how it should be parried, and how, if the opponent of the one using it were quick, and could depend upon his wrist, a counter-thrust quite as dangerous could be delivered.

Though I had never put into practice what I had seen demonstrated, since occasion had never before arisen, I resolved to attempt it now, for I felt sure von Ettergarde would presently try the ruse again, his first attempt having fallen so little short of success. Indeed, I believe he thought my fate was as good as sealed, for a little smile began to hover about his mouth. There was some further cautious play on both sides, and then I again advanced a pace, giving my antagonist, as he supposed, the desired opportunity to execute his coup. But this time my blade met and turned aside his forward thrust, was carried by a quick straightening of my arm upward, pierced his neck just above the dip where the clavicle and the breast-bone join, and came out at the base of his skull. My sword was wrenched from my hand as he fell forward. I caught a glimpse of the horror of his contorted face; then Hartzheim came in through the casement and embraced me, calling me I know not what extravagant names, filling my ears with praise, bidding me go to Angela, and saying that he would follow in a moment and bring me my sword.

Soon my beloved's arms were about me, and then I came nigh to playing the woman; but Hartzheim saved me by appearing just at the right moment and announcing that there was still much to be done before we could afford to waste time in love-making.

Undetected we **gained** the balcony of the unoccupied house, pried open one of the casements, **and were** soon threading the streets in the direction of the **Porta** Venezia. Fortunately not a soul was abroad. With the breaking of dawn the watchmen had retired to their homes, and it was yet too early either for the hardiest laborer or the most enterprising vender to be stirring.

Our only **fear now was that** orders had been issued to **allow no** one answering **to our description to leave** the **city,** but von Ettergarde, who doubtless had but **just** arrived when we heard his summons at the house of the Canari hard upon midnight, had failed to take any such precautions. Although the gate-keeper grumbled at being disturbed, and seemed curious to see folk of our evident station on foot at such an hour, he readily opened the gates for us after I had slipped something yellow and glistening into his hand, and Hartzheim had explained that we purposed to go hawking, and looked to find our servants and hawks and horses awaiting us at the Three Kings.

Galbo was quickly roused and the horses saddled, and then as the sun-rays were dispelling the last vestiges of the night, the brooding vapors, and the low-lying mists, we galloped away from Brescia through the fresh air of the morning, and long ere noon passed in safety from the territory of the Visconti into that of Francesco da Gonzaga, the Marquis of Mantua.

For each of us that day ushered in a new life. To Signor Canaro, despite the loss of his princely home, came a peace, a security, and a contentment which he had not known for years, a world of quiet pleasure in the society of those he loved, and in the companionship of one who, like himself, had felt the cruelty of sorrow and misfortune,— my cousin, Alberto Gambacorta. To Hartzheim came abundance and prosperity, the cosy inn of his choice, and the little woman of his heart seated as mistress by his fireside. Truly nothing was too good for one who, at the sacrifice of his own position and interests, had done so much for friendship's sake, and to see the right prevail! To Angela and myself came a great and ever-abiding happiness, — a happiness which grows sweeter and sweeter as the pilgrim years slip away.

Never again were any of us enmeshed in the Great Viper's coils (Venice offering a safe asylum when, for a time, Padua fell under the sway of the Visconti), but not until more than half a score of years after our outriding from Brescia that memorable morning did the long-delaying hand of fate smite down the man who was a terror to prince and peasant. During the summer of 1402, the plague descended upon Lombardy with fatal fury. To the barred gates of the isolated fortress of Marignano it at last found its way. Where human foot could not gain an entrance in it crept, stole from room to room, and finally found one in a sequestered apartment cringing and shaking with cowardly fear. It leaped upon him, gripped him by the throat, and when the news spread abroad through Italy, a great shout of deliverance went up, for a curse that was worse than the plague had been lifted from the land.

THE END